Cassie Comes Through

Cassie Comes Through

Shana Muldoon Zappa and Ahmet Zappa

with Zelda Rose

Disney•Press

Los Angeles • New York

Printed in the United States of America
Reinforced Binding
First Paperback Edition, February 2016
1 3 5 7 9 10 8 6 4 2

FAC-025438-15352

Library of Congress Control Number: 2015953723
ISBN 978-1-4847-1425-6

To our beautiful, sweet treasure,
Halo Violetta Zappa. You are pure light and joy
and our greatest inspiration. We love you soooo much.

May every step upon your path be blessed with positivity and
the understanding that you have the power within you to
manifest the most fulfilling life you can possibly imagine and
more. May you always remember that being different and true
to your highest self makes your inner star shine brighter.

Remember that you have the power of choice. . . . Choose thoughts
that feel good. Choose love and friendship that feed your spirit.
Choose actions for peace and nourishment. Choose boundaries
for the same. Choose what speaks to your creativity and unique
inner voice . . . what truly makes you happy. And always know
that no matter what you choose, you are unconditionally loved.

Look up to the stars and know you are never alone.
When in doubt, go within . . . the answers are all there.
Smiles light the world and laughter is the best medicine.
And NEVER EVER stop making wishes. . . .

Glow for it. . . .
Mommy and Daddy

And to everyone else here on "Wishworld":

May you realize that no matter where you are in life, no
matter what you look like or where you were born, you, too,
have the power within you to create the life of your dreams.
Through celebrating your own uniqueness, thinking positively,
and taking action, you can make your wishes come true.

Smile. The Star Darlings have your back.
We know how startastic you truly are.

Glow for it. . . .
Your friends,
Shana and Ahmet

Student Reports

NAME: Clover
BRIGHT DAY: January 5
FAVORITE COLOR: Purple
INTERESTS: Music, painting, studying
WISH: To be the best songwriter and DJ on Starland
WHY CHOSEN: Clover has great self-discipline, patience, and willpower. She is creative, responsible, dependable, and extremely loyal.
WATCH OUT FOR: Clover can be hard to read and she is reserved with those she doesn't know. She's afraid to take risks and can be a wisecracker at times.
SCHOOL YEAR: Second
POWER CRYSTAL: Panthera
WISH PENDANT: Barrette

* * * * * * * * * * *

NAME: Adora
BRIGHT DAY: February 14
FAVORITE COLOR: Sky blue
INTERESTS: Science, thinking about the future and how she can make it better
WISH: To be the top fashion designer on Starland
WHY CHOSEN: Adora is clever and popular and cares about the world around her. She's a deep thinker.
WATCH OUT FOR: Adora can have her head in the clouds and be thinking about other things.
SCHOOL YEAR: Third
POWER CRYSTAL: Azurica
WISH PENDANT: Watch

* * * * * * * * * * *

NAME: Piper
BRIGHT DAY: March 4
FAVORITE COLOR: Seafoam green
INTERESTS: Composing poetry and writing in her dream journal
WISH: To become the best version of herself she can possibly be and to share that by writing books
WHY CHOSEN: Piper is giving, kind, and sensitive. She is very intuitive and aware.
WATCH OUT FOR: Piper can be dreamy, absentminded, and wishy-washy. She can also be moody and easily swayed by the opinions of others.
SCHOOL YEAR: Second
POWER CRYSTAL: Dreamalite
WISH PENDANT: Bracelets

Starling Academy

NAME: Astra
BRIGHT DAY: April 9
FAVORITE COLOR: Red
INTERESTS: Individual sports
WISH: To be the best athlete on Starland—to win!
WHY CHOSEN: Astra is energetic, brave, clever, and confident. She has boundless energy and is always direct and to the point.
WATCH OUT FOR: Astra is sometimes cocky, self-centered, condescending, and brash.
SCHOOL YEAR: Second
POWER CRYSTAL: Quarrelite
WISH PENDANT: Wristbands

* * * * * * * * * *

NAME: Tessa
BRIGHT DAY: May 18
FAVORITE COLOR: Emerald green
INTERESTS: Food, flowers, love
WISH: To be successful enough that she can enjoy a life of luxury
WHY CHOSEN: Tessa is warm, charming, affectionate, trustworthy, and dependable. She has incredible drive and commitment.
WATCH OUT FOR: Tessa does not like to be rushed. She can be quite stubborn and often says no. She does not deal well with change and is prone to exaggeration. She can be easily sidetracked.
SCHOOL YEAR: Third
POWER CRYSTAL: Gossamer
WISH PENDANT: Brooch

* * * * * * * * * *

NAME: Gemma
BRIGHT DAY: June 2
FAVORITE COLOR: Orange
INTERESTS: Sharing her thoughts about almost anything
WISH: To be valued for her opinions on everything
WHY CHOSEN: Gemma is friendly, easygoing, funny, extroverted, and social. She knows a little bit about everything.
WATCH OUT FOR: Gemma talks—a lot—and can be a little too honest sometimes and offend others. She can have a short attention span and can be superficial.
SCHOOL YEAR: First
POWER CRYSTAL: Scatterite
WISH PENDANT: Earrings

Student Reports

NAME: Cassie
BRIGHT DAY: July 6
FAVORITE COLOR: White
INTERESTS: Reading, crafting
WISH: To be more independent and confident and less fearful
WHY CHOSEN: Cassie is extremely imaginative and artistic. She is a voracious reader and is loyal, caring, and a good friend. She is very intuitive.
WATCH OUT FOR: Cassie can be distrustful, jealous, moody, and brooding.
SCHOOL YEAR: First
POWER CRYSTAL: Lunalite
WISH PENDANT: Glasses

* • • *• • *• • *• • *

NAME: Leona
BRIGHT DAY: August 16
FAVORITE COLOR: Gold
INTERESTS: Acting, performing, dressing up
WISH: To be the most famous pop star on Starland
WHY CHOSEN: Leona is confident, hardworking, generous, open-minded, optimistic, caring, and a strong leader.
WATCH OUT FOR: Leona can be vain, opinionated, selfish, bossy, dramatic, and stubborn and is prone to losing her temper.
SCHOOL YEAR: Third
POWER CRYSTAL: Glisten paw
WISH PENDANT: Cuff

* • • *• • *• • *• • *

NAME: Vega
BRIGHT DAY: September 1
FAVORITE COLOR: Blue
INTERESTS: Exercising, analyzing, cleaning, solving puzzles
WISH: To be the top student at Starling Academy
WHY CHOSEN: Vega is reliable, observant, organized, and very focused.
WATCH OUT FOR: Vega can be opinionated about everything, and she can be fussy, uptight, critical, arrogant, and easily embarrassed.
SCHOOL YEAR: Second
POWER CRYSTAL: Queezle
WISH PENDANT: Belt

Starling Academy

NAME: Libby
BRIGHT DAY: October 12
FAVORITE COLOR: Pink
INTERESTS: Helping others, interior design, art, dancing
WISH: To give everyone what they need—both on Starland and through wish granting on Wishworld
WHY CHOSEN: Libby is generous, articulate, gracious, diplomatic, and kind.
WATCH OUT FOR: Libby can be indecisive and may try too hard to please everyone.
SCHOOL YEAR: First
POWER CRYSTAL: Charmelite
WISH PENDANT: Necklace

* · · * · · · ★ · · * · · *

NAME: Scarlet
BRIGHT DAY: November 3
FAVORITE COLOR: Black
INTERESTS: Crystal climbing (and other extreme sports), magic, thrill seeking
WISH: To live on Wishworld
WHY CHOSEN: Scarlet is confident, intense, passionate, magnetic, curious, and very brave.
WATCH OUT FOR: Scarlet is a loner and can alienate others by being secretive, arrogant, stubborn, and jealous.
SCHOOL YEAR: Third
POWER CRYSTAL: Ravenstone
WISH PENDANT: Boots

* · · * · · · ★ · · * · · *

NAME: Sage
BRIGHT DAY: December 1
FAVORITE COLOR: Lavender
INTERESTS: Travel, adventure, telling stories, nature, and philosophy
WISH: To become the best Wish-Granter Starland has ever seen
WHY CHOSEN: Sage is honest, adventurous, curious, optimistic, friendly, and relaxed.
WATCH OUT FOR: Sage has a quick temper! She can also be restless, irresponsible, and too trusting of others' opinions. She may jump to conclusions.
SCHOOL YEAR: First
POWER CRYSTAL: Lavenderite
WISH PENDANT: Necklace

Introduction

You take a deep breath, about to blow out the candles on your birthday cake. Clutching a coin in your fist, you get ready to toss it into the dancing waters of a fountain. You stare at your little brother as you each hold an end of a dried wishbone, about to pull. But what do you do first?

You make a wish, of course!

Ever wonder what happens right after you make that wish? *Not much*, you may be thinking.

Well, you'd be wrong.

Because something quite unexpected happens next. Each and every wish that is made becomes a glowing Wish Orb, invisible to the human eye. This undetectable orb zips through the air and into the heavens, on a one-way trip to the brightest star in the sky—a magnificent place called Starland. Starland is inhabited by Starlings, who look a lot like you and me, except they have a sparkly glow to their skin, and glittery hair in unique colors. And they have one more thing: magical powers. The Starlings use these powers to make good wishes come true, for when good wishes are granted, the result is positive energy. And the Starlings of Starland need this energy to keep their world running.

In case you are wondering, there are three kinds of Wish Orbs:

1) GOOD WISH ORBS. These wishes are positive and helpful and come from the heart. They are pretty and sparkly and are nurtured in climate-controlled Wish-Houses. They bloom into fantastical glowing orbs. When the time is right, they are presented to the appropriate Starling for wish fulfillment.

2) BAD WISH ORBS. These are for selfish, mean-spirited, or negative things. They don't sparkle

at all. They are immediately transported to a special containment center, as they are very dangerous and must not be granted.

3) IMPOSSIBLE WISH ORBS. These wishes are for things, like world peace and disease cures, that simply can't be granted by Starlings. These sparkle with an almost impossibly bright light and are taken to a special area of the Wish-House with tinted windows to contain the glare they produce. The hope is that one day they can be turned into good wishes the Starlings can help grant.

Starlings take their wish granting very seriously. There is a special school, called Starling Academy, that accepts only the best and brightest young Starling girls. They study hard for four years, and when they graduate, they are ready to start traveling to Wishworld to help grant wishes. For as long as anyone can remember, only graduates of wish-granting schools have ever been allowed to travel to Wishworld. But things have changed in a very big way.

Read on for the rest of the story. . . .

Prologue

 You there, Vega?

 I'm here, Cassie. In the maze with Scarlet waiting for you!

 ???

 Didn't you get my holo-text?

 That's so weird. I didn't get it. You know I hate that maze, anyway. Can we just talk now?

Sure. I'll add Scarlet.

 Hey, Cassie.

 Hey, Scarlet! Starkudos on your Wish Mission!

 Star salutations! It wasn't easy, that's for sure.

 So I just told Scarlet we found out that the flowers that were delivered to the Star Darlings are from the Isle of Misera!

 Crazy! No wonder everyone was fighting so much. But I thought that place was off-limits. Who do you think sent them? And why?

 That's a very good question. And as a matter of fact, that's not the only strange thing going on at Starling Academy . . .

 You mean the way I was kicked out of the group and replaced by Ophelia? And then had to go down to Wishworld to save her stars?

 Yes, plus I just finished Vega's crossword puzzle . . .

Star salutations! I'm impressed! So, what did you think?

It's pretty starmazing!

 I had to make some changes and move some answers around to get it to line up so perfectly. I'm glad you enjoyed it!

 Um, yeah, it was a startastic layout . . .

 but I was talking about the actual content.

 I mean, when I saw all those the clues together, it was eye-opening!

Spit it out, Cassie!

 Think about it! Look at 3-Across, 7-Across, and sorry, your mission, too, Vega—everyone has had a problem identifying either her Wisher or the wish. And 10-Across: Leona's private band tryout invite got holo-blasted to the entire school and our top-secret name was revealed. Or how about 8-Down: Leona's Wish Pendant got ruined and she didn't collect any wish energy.

Plus me, Ophelia, the flowers . . .

1) I l♥ve, l♥ve, l♥ve that my puzzle got you thinking, Cassie! 2) Wow. I was only looking at them as puzzle clues. But when you actually read them one after another, it's pretty crazy!

 Starzactly.

 There is a lot of weird stuff going on, that's for sure. And what about my and Ophelia's deliberately switched grades?

 Was that ever proven?

 Well, not yet, but . . .

 Listen, we need to stay calm. Do you think it could just be a coincidence?

 No way!

 Well . . . we've been brought together to do something so controversial it has to be kept secret from everyone else at Starling Academy— to collect wish energy on Wishworld before we graduate. I'm afraid that maybe we're being sanitized.

 ???

Okay, now I'm really confused!

 Darn you, starcorrect! I meant sabotaged!

 That's terrible! But . . . by who?

 Okay, I don't know how to say this. I know you think I can be paranoid. . . .

 Um, well, maybe because just yesterday you were convinced that someone stole your starglasses, and they were sitting on top of your head!

  Okay, so maybe you have a point. But . . .

 Yes?

 Well, um, what if someone really is out to get us? What better way to do it . . .

 Waiting . . .

 . . . than from within? What if it is someone here at Starling Academy? Or even worse . . .

 What could be worse?

 What if it's one of us . . . a Star Darling???

 I hope you're wrong . . .

And if I'm not?

 Then there's only one thing to say: Oh, starf.

 You said it, Starling.

CHAPTER
1

"Well, there you are, Bitty!" Cassie cooed as her pet glowfur landed on her shoulder and nuzzled her pale cheek. Bitty's soft pink fur tickled Cassie's face and made the tiny girl giggle. Cassie smiled at the little creature in the mirror as she finished twisting her long, glimmering pinkish-white hair into a second pigtail bun, fastened it in place with a starpin, and reached up to give the creature a quick tickle. Bitty chirped delightedly and the stars on her golden antennae twinkled. The glowfur rewarded Cassie with the "Song of Contentment." Cassie, who had heard it many times before, hummed along.

"That's really pretty," someone said. Cassie turned around to find her roommate smiling at her. Sage, freshly gleaming from her sparkle shower, was wrapped in a soft lavender towel that matched her hair and eyes.

Cassie nodded in agreement. "Can you believe that glowfurs have twenty-six distinct songs?" she asked. "And that each glowfur has her own version of each tune? This is one of my favorites. After the 'Song of Joy' and 'Song of Enchantment,' of course."

"Yes, I can believe it," said Sage. "Only because you've told me a moonium times!"

Although Cassie's first impulse was to scowl at Sage, she just rolled her eyes and laughed instead. That was the key to having a pleasant relationship with her roommate. Cassie was beginning to realize that Sage didn't mean to offend; she just liked to say whatever was on her mind.

Sage opened her closet door with her wish energy manipulation skills and quickly got dressed behind it. When she emerged, she was wearing a loosely woven shimmery sweater over a long sleeveless dress that flickered and changed color as she moved—exhibiting more shades of purple than Cassie knew existed. Cassie preferred to wear more delicate outfits, mostly in white and pale shades of silver and pink, but she appreciated the bold color of Sage's flowing, comfortable clothes. Sage shook her head in mock seriousness. "Actually, what I really can't believe is you still haven't gotten caught," she said with a laugh.

"That's because Bitty and I are very careful," said Cassie, smoothing her silvery tunic with the ruffled hem. Bitty took off from Cassie's shoulder and circled the room, still singing her song. Cassie smiled at Sage. "And because I have a very discreet roommate."

Sage nodded from the floor, where she crouched, buckling her sparkly sandals. "I *am* discreet, aren't I?"

"You are," said Cassie. She poured Bitty's daily allotment of Green Globules into a crystal bowl and Bitty zoomed over, her bright blue gossamer wings fluttering madly as they struggled to hold up the weight of her plump little body. She knocked over a pile of holo-books in her rush to enjoy her breakfast. Cassie had read the Starling Academy Student Manual from cover to cover and knew quite well that pets were expressly forbidden to live in the student dormitories. She told herself that she had taken Bitty to school with her because the creature would have been lonely back at her uncle Andreas's

couldn't part with her pet, who had once belonged to Cassie's late mother. When Bitty sang her evening song,

Cassie was reminded that her mother had fallen asleep to the very same tune many staryears ago. It wasn't much, in the grand scheme of things, but it brought her great comfort. So Cassie had packed up Bitty and her various glowfur paraphernalia and successfully smuggled her past the Bot-Bot guards on the first day of school.

But keeping Bitty a secret from her roommate had not been easy. There had been that unpleasant moment when, to avoid suspicion, she had to eat a Green Globule after Sage's nosy little brothers had found a bag of them under her bed. Her face wrinkled up at the distasteful memory. And there had been the time when Sage woke to Bitty's singing and tried to convince Cassie that she and her "stellar voice" needed to join the starchoir. (Cassie's voice was actually quite mediocre, so she had feigned a sore throat, missing tryouts.) But it turned out that Sage had already guessed Cassie's secret and accepted her small and furry extra roommate. Cassie had had another stressful period during the time when she and Sage hadn't been getting along and she had grown nervous that her roommate might turn her in. But Sage had proved to be a loyal roommate, even when the two were bickering.

It was those flowers! thought Cassie, staring at the spot where the vase had sat, its coral blooms fragrant, enticing, and perpetually fresh and dewy. But Cassie

had had a feeling that something was not quite right with them, and her hunches were often correct. There was suddenly a lot of tension in the room, and Cassie had realized that she could just not get along with her roommate. In a moment of impulse, she had grabbed the flowers and tossed them into the vanishing garbage can, and things had returned to normal between them. And then she had convinced Vega that they should bring *her* flowers to the botany lab. They had discovered that the flowers came from the Isle of Misera, a place off-limits to Starlings. But who had sent them? And why? That was still a mystery. Cassie made it her mission to destroy the rest of the flowers, but it wasn't easy. She had tried to explain to the rest of the Star Darlings that the flowers were having a bad effect on them, but everyone had just laughed. She had a theory that the longer someone kept the flowers, the more attached to them that person became, so she'd had to get creative. On her fingers, she ticked off the roommate pairs who no longer had flowers in their rooms. Vega and Piper's flowers were still

of a heated argument over who had forgotten to turn off the sparkle shower. She had only been able to convince Tessa to get rid of the flowers once she told her that their strong odor interfered with the delicious smells of her baking. And Leona and Ophelia's had simply disappeared. (She still hadn't figured that one out, but at least they were gone.) That left one roommate pair who still had the flowers in their room—Clover and Astra. Cassie needed to get right on that as soon as starpossible.

Sage finished buckling her sandals and walked to the door, her lavender braids gleaming.

"Ready to go to the Celestial Café?" she asked Cassie.

"Ready!" said Cassie. Bitty zoomed in for a kiss on her furry head and began her good-bye song.

Cassie hurried to the door. "Oh, let me," she begged, so Sage stepped aside. Cassie concentrated on opening the door with her wish energy manipulation skills and the door began to tremble, almost imperceptibly, as if it was trying to decide whether it wanted to be opened or stay closed. A starmin or two later, after Cassie's pale face flushed silver from the effort, the door slid open fluidly.

Cassie grinned and turned to Sage. "You're like my good-luck charm, Sage," she said. "I wish I was as good in Wish Energy Manipulation class as I am in our room." She shrugged. "I guess I get stage fright or something."

Sage nodded and for a starsec Cassie thought she caught a small flicker of a smile on her roommate's face.

But it disappeared as they stepped into the hallway and onto the Cosmic Transporter.

Cassie's stomach grumbled. "I wonder what to order for break—" she started.

"Stop right there!" a voice barked.

Cassie sighed. They were moving along on the Cosmic Transporter and couldn't stop even if they wanted to, for stars' sake. But Sage laughed merrily. "Hurry up, MO-Jay!" she cried.

The Bot-Bot guide zoomed after them eagerly. His official name was MO-J4, but Sage thought that was a little too formal and had settled on the nickname, which he had embraced wholeheartedly. MO-Jay had taken an instant starshine to Sage during her orientation tour and had been delighted by anything Sage did or said ever since. Most Bot-Bots acted by the holo-book with a preset vocabulary and a limited range of programmed reactions. But MO-Jay was special. He had a personality that was silly and fun, and he often greeted Sage with special jokes and an occasional gift left on her doorstep

rise and showed her a holo-vid he had taken of it just for her. Sometimes Cassie wished that she and Bitty could talk, like Sage and MO-Jay did. Though she wasn't quite sure what Bitty would say. Most likely "More Green Globules, please." Or maybe "Rub my glowbelly for another starhour if you don't mind." The only present Bitty had ever given her (besides the gift of music) was a half-eaten Green Globule, left in the toe of a silver slipper. And by the time Cassie had found it, it was as hard as a meteorite. Cassie had tossed it into the vanishing garbage can. She knew exactly what Green Globules tasted like, even at the peak of freshness: horrible.

Still, she wouldn't trade Bitty for all the wish energy in Starland. She half listened to Sage and Mojo chat away. She smiled, remembering that Sage had initially confided to her that she found MO-J4's slavish devotion a bit annoying. But then the silvery Bot-Bot had started to grow on her. Sage told Cassie she was used to small annoying creatures, referring to her younger twin brothers, who could be quite a handful. As an only child, and an orphaned one at that, Cassie had nodded in apparent sympathy. But Cassie would actually have liked nothing more than an annoying sibling (or two or even three) to liven things up around her uncle's quiet home. That was why she liked Starling Academy so much, she realized. It was lively and there was always something going on to keep her entertained. Like that time when Astra had bet everyone that she could do a triple flip off the starbounce while eating a half-moon pie. It looked like she was going to win the wager when Leona had jumped up and—

Just then she realized that Sage was trying to get her attention. "Cassie!" she was saying, snapping her fingers in Cassie's face. Cassie blinked. "We haven't even discussed the new Scarlet situation yet!" she said. "I mean, that was so unexpected. So what do you think about her reinsta—"

Cassie held up her hand. She turned to MO-J4. "I'm going to remind you that everything you hear is strictly confidential," she told the Bot-Bot. Even though he was extremely devoted to Sage, the Star Darlings couldn't risk anyone's—or anybot's—leaking information about their secret mission.

MO-J4's eyes flashed as if he was annoyed, or perhaps disappointed, by the request, but he politely nodded. "Certainly, Cassie," he said smoothly.

Sage nodded solemnly. "So what do you think about Scarlet's reinstatement?" she asked. "It's just so strange,"

Scarlet had promised Vega that until they had some more evidence they would keep to themselves their fears about what they thought was going on. No need to throw everyone else into a tizzy if there was a reasonable explanation for everything, Vega had argued. Cassie and Scarlet had reluctantly agreed.

"Well, it was certainly a sur—" she finally started.

"I think it's simply wonderful!" MO-J4 exclaimed. "Now the group can get back together and you can win the Battle of the Bands on Starshine Day. Beat that Vivica, just like she deserves!"

"All right, see you later, MO-Jay," she said. They had reached the Celestial Café. The light was shining above the door. Breakfast was ready to be served and another day was about to unfold.

Sage smiled at Cassie. "And our starday begins," she said. "Hope it's a good one."

Cassie tapped her elbows together three times for luck. She herself was hoping for a day filled with more clues. Something strange was going on at Starling Academy; she was almost sure of it. She just needed some tangible proof.

CHAPTER
2

"**How many times** do I have to tell you?" Clover scolded her roommate. "No star balls at the breakfast table!" She rolled her eyes, turning to the rest of the Star Darlings sitting around the table as if she was an exasperated teacher and Astra a naughty Wee Constellation School student. "She throws that thing around all day long. It never stops. It's driving me crazy! I wake up in the middle of the night and there she is, tossing that ball!"

"I told you, Coach Geeta said we have to practice as

matching glittery spots appeared on her cheeks. Cassie knew Astra well enough to know that meant she was getting angry.

"I'm sure she didn't mean in the Celestial Café!" Clover practically shouted. The rest of the Star Darlings looked at each other uncomfortably. The usually fun-loving Clover was being very rigid, and Astra was being way more stubborn than usual. It wasn't enjoyable to watch the two butt heads so forcefully. Cassie held her breath as Astra grinned wickedly and tossed the shining orb into the air again, her hands poised to catch it. She made the ball hover in the air over the table for a moment, showing off the skills that made her Starling Academy's most talented star ball player. Just then a Bot-Bot waiter zoomed in with a breakfast tray.

"Yum!" said Astra, distracted for a moment. "Am I hungry! I had quite a workout this morning!" And Cassie watched in shock as the shining orb crashed down, faster than she thought possible. "Oh, my stars!" said the Bot-Bot in dismay as it hit his tray with a loud smack, sending stacks of steaming starcakes and glasses of glorange juice flying onto the table.

The girls stared at the scattered starcakes and the puddles of glowing glorange juice on the fancy table-cloth. Tessa, who hated to see any food go to waste, quickly snatched up a starcake and took a bite out of one of its perfect five points. Clover looked furious. The rest of the girls exchanged glances. They knew Clover was overreacting, since the mess immediately disappeared, as messes always did on Starland. "Pardon me," said the Bot-Bot apologetically as he neatly stacked the plates and zoomed back to the kitchen for a replacement breakfast tray. Cassie nudged Vega's leg under the table. But the girl didn't react. Cassie did it again.

"Did you just kick me?" Astra scowled across the table at Clover.

Oops, thought Cassie.

"No, I didn't!" Clover retorted. "But maybe I should!"

The two girls glared at each other. Cassie noticed that although both their mouths were set in grim lines, there were matching looks of confusion in their eyes. It was as if they couldn't understand why they were so angry at each other, and they weren't very happy about it, either.

That's it, thought Cassie. If there had been any question in her mind about the negative effect of the vases of flowers, it had just been answered. Everyone else was getting along well (with the exception of Leona and

and Scarlet had to come up with a plan to dispose of the flowers—that starday.

The rest of breakfast went by without incident, and

Cassie leapt up from the table as soon as she took her last bite of astromuffin. She hurried out of the cafeteria, excited to get to her first class of the day—Intro to Wish Identification. Never slowing her pace, she hopped onto the Cosmic Transporter that looped through campus, and she jumped off at Halo Hall. She bounded up the steps and through the large imposing doors, which dwarfed her tiny figure. Although Cassie's secret Star Darlings lessons had placed her far beyond the rest of the first-year class, and she often found boring the introductory lessons she had to attend to keep up her cover, she was really looking forward to that day's class. They were going to attempt wish identification on a Starlandian creature. Cassie tapped her elbows together three times for luck, hoping they'd be studying a glion or a galliope, or maybe even a twinkelope. She would love to hear its trumpeting call in person. Being up close with any one of those majestic creatures would really be a thrill, as would trying to figure out what its wish could possibly be. She quickened her pace down the comfortable hallway, toward the wish stellation. She didn't want to be late.

"Cassie, wait up!"

Now what? thought Cassie as she abruptly stopped, the soles of her silvery ankle boots squeaking on the floor. She turned around impatiently. But her scowl disappeared. To her starprise, it was Leona pushing through the crowd of students to get to her side. *Imagine that.*

"I need to catch my breath!" Leona gasped, putting her sparkly golden hand to her sparkly golden throat. "You practically ran right out of the Celestial Café. I've been chasing you ever since!"

"You look really glowful," said Cassie appreciatively, taking in the girl's aura. Leona had been looking decidedly unglimmery ever since her failed mission. That had concerned all the Star Darlings, since Leona was naturally extra golden to begin with.

"Star salutations," said Leona, holding out a sparkly arm and admiring it. "I'm starting to feel a bit better."

"I'm glad," said Cassie, and she really meant it. It felt good to be talking to Leona. Sure, they had been in Star Darlings class together and seated at the Star Darlings' table at the dining hall, but this was the first time they were talking one-on-one since their argument about Ophelia.

friends had starprised her. Cassie had initially felt intimidated by the bold, brash third year, never in a moonium staryears dreaming that the two would have anything in common—or that she would actually enjoy spending time with a girl who seemed always on the lookout for an admiring audience. Cassie had assumed that Leona would be exhausting to be around, but the truth was that Leona's zest for life ⁀nergized and inspired her. And she learned that Leona had a kind and generous side that was easy to overlook at first glance.

Their unlikely friendship had begun one evening on the way back from dinner shortly after school had started. The Star Darlings were on the Cosmic Transporter heading back to their dormitories. Cassie recalled that Leona was singing a song about the beauty of lightfall, her arms thrown out and her eyes closed. Cassie thought that the girl looked more luminous than anyone else, her golden hair a brilliant halo around her radiant face. She was shocked when Leona had impulsively grabbed her hand at the end of the song. "We're going to the roof," Leona had announced, and before Cassie could argue, she had whisked her into the upperclassman dormitory and up onto the roof deck. Cassie, who had thought she preferred always being in the background, was surprised to discover she enjoyed being in the golden spotlight of Leona's attention. The two girls had lain on lounge chairs well into the night, staring at the magnificently star-studded sky, squealing when they spotted a shooting star. They pointed out constellations to each other, and when they ran out of names, they made some up. Leona told Cassie all about her family, about how she loved them fiercely but sometimes felt held back by their limited view of the world. And Leona had been the first person at Starling Academy who Cassie had told about her parents, tentatively pointing out their stars, which winked at her as they always did. Leona had known that no words were required at that moment, just a warm hand to hold as they sat in silence and stared into the heavens. The two didn't realize how late it was until they saw how the stars had completely shifted across the sky. Cassie had had to sneak back into her dorm long after lights-out. In fact, she had felt a little thrill of naughtiness when she'd placed her hand on her room's palm scanner and the Bot-Bot voice had said, "Good evening, Cassie," in what she was certain was a disapproving tone.

But her friendship with Leona had practically ground to a halt after the Starling's disastrous mission. While Cassie understood how disappointed Leona was when it was discovered that she had not collected any wish energy, she was surprised when Leona had completely shut down and frozen her out. Instead Leona had chosen to spend time with her new roommate, and Scarlet's replacement as a Star Darling, Ophelia. And once Cassie had started asking questions about Ophelia—who, everyone agreed, didn't seem to be Star Darlings material at all—Leona had taken great offense. They had pretty much avoided being alone together ever since.

Sure, Cassie felt a slight glimmer of resentment that Leona had dropped her friendship so abruptly, but her delight in seeing her friend looking so much better won out. Leona gave her a blinding megawatt smile and Cassie grinned right back. All right, maybe Leona's smile wasn't *quite* as intense as it had been before all her mission troubles, but it was still pretty dazzling.

Leona slipped her arm through Cassie's. She leaned down as if to tell Cassie a secret. "So can you believe it?" she whispered, her breath tickling Cassie's ear. "You know they moved Ophelia into the Little Dipper Dormitory. Not only did I lose the sweetest roommate ever, but I'm sharing a room with weird old Scarlet again."

"Poor you," said Cassie, feeling a stab of guilt. She was fond of Scarlet—or as fond as anyone could be of the secretive and somewhat strange girl. But her pleasure at being back in Leona's good graces outweighed her loyalty to Scarlet.

"All that black!" Leona groaned. "And the constant skateboarding messing up my beauty sleep. And remember, she plays the *drums* and she always forgets to turn on the muting switch. And her weird stuff lying around. Globerbeem cases and old meepletile skins. Ugh." She shuddered with distaste. "Imagine what new oddities she's collected since I've seen her last." She sighed and made a sad face. "And what's going to happen to Ophelia? She may not be a Star Darling, but she's such a sweet Starling." She gave Cassie a sidelong glance and her eyes widened. "You know something? She's an orphan, too! But she has no one at all, not like you with your famous uncle to take care of you. As a matter of fact, she grew up in an orphanage in Starland City. She hadn't made any friends in Starling Academy until she met me. And now she's all alone again."

"Oh," said Cassie. She hadn't known that about Ophelia. She had been so focused on the wrongness of Ophelia's being a Star Darling that it hadn't occurred to her to think about the girl's feelings. Now all Cassie felt was sympathy for her. No one but a fellow orphan could understand the unspeakable pain of losing both of your parents at a young age. Of feeling so achingly alone, like you belonged to no one, adrift in a world that was suddenly empty and terribly frightening. And the devastating realization that life would never, ever be the same. For a girl who was searching for a place to fit in, being offered the chance to be a part of a secret group and then having it suddenly taken away must have been devastating.

Cassie swallowed hard. "I . . . I . . . I'll keep an eye out for her," she heard herself say.

"And you'll talk to her, see how she's doing?" Leona pressed.

Cassie nodded. "I will. Cross my stars and hope to shine."

"Star salutations," said Leona. "I'm worried about her. I really am."

Cassie nodded. "Well, here's my classroom," she said. She unlinked her arm from Leona's and impulsively gave her a quick hug. She tried to step back, but Leona held on for a moment longer than Cassie was expecting.

Leona had missed her. And that was a pretty nice thing to realize.

CHAPTER
3

When Cassie stepped inside, she saw that her classmates were clustered together in the front of the room. *Professor Lucretia Delphinus is either teaching the class how to shoot holo-dice or the Starlandian creature's already here,* she thought with a grin. But she had no one to share her little joke with. Cassie had a well-deserved reputation as a quiet girl who liked her privacy and never spoke out of turn, and her classmates respected this and tended to leave her alone.

She was okay with that. *Still,* she thought as she stood uncertainly at the front of the class, *it would be nice if someone would turn around and say hello or move over to make room for me in the circle.* But she wasn't surprised that no one did. What was disappointing to her was that she knew her fellow classmates (and sometimes professors, as well) often took her reserved nature for aloofness or, worse yet, thought she had nothing to contribute. She did have a lot to offer; it was just that she liked to get all her thoughts in order before she opened her mouth. She didn't like idle chitchat, throwaway comments, or speaking for the sole purpose of hearing herself talk. She couldn't fathom being like Gemma, who could make small talk with anyone—teachers, students, parents, staff, strangers. Gemma was quite well liked because of it. But Cassie found the girl's constant chatter simply exhausting.

The one place Cassie truly felt at ease was among her fellow Star Darlings. They seemed to appreciate her thoughtful, deliberate responses and had learned never to rush her to speak her mind before she was ready. She felt as if she had found her place. That's why all the strange things that were going on were making her feel extra nervous. How she hoped it wasn't a fellow Star Darling who was responsible. *That is*, if *anything is going on*, she reminded herself, hearing Vega's voice of reason in her head. There could be a logical explanation for everything, couldn't there?

The crowd of students hadn't shifted an inch. Cassie stood on her toes to try to peer over them, but as she expected, it was useless. She overheard snippets of conversation: "How startastic!" and "I can't wait to guess what the wish is!" She bit her lip in anticipation.

"Okay, class, time to get started," Professor Lucretia Delphinus called out. "Everyone to your seats."

The girls reluctantly scattered and Cassie headed to her desk. She plopped down into the chair, which immediately adjusted to her height, build, and preferred seating position, the ultimate in classroom comfort. Vega had told her that the seats in Wishworld classrooms were hard and rigid. That didn't make sense to Cassie at all. She couldn't imagine how you could pay attention to your lessons when you were uncomfortable.

Now that the students were all seated, Cassie was frustrated when she realized that she still couldn't see the creature. Her professor, a tiny woman in a voluminous swirly purple-and-blue skirt that looked like a moonstorm, was somehow positioned in a way that precisely blocked her view. She craned her neck, but she was unable to see behind the woman.

"Star greetings, students," said Professor Lucretia Delphinus. "Welcome to your first wish identification workshop. Today we will be granting the wishes of our special guest, Mica." She stepped to the side and Cassie finally caught a glimpse. The creature was sitting in the middle of the teacher's desk, staring into space. Cassie felt her spirits drop. It wasn't a majestic glion who could be wishing to climb to the top of the Crystal Mountains and graze on the rainbow lichen that grew there or a galliope who might want to take a lucky student for a ride on his broad back, her fingers laced through his glittering mane. She would not be hearing the bellowing call of the many-antlered twinkelope anytime soon. No, that day they would be guessing the wishes of a much smaller and decidedly less glamorous creature—a creature Cassie knew almost as well as she knew herself: a glowfur.

Cassie shook her head and laughed to herself. This wasn't going to be challenging at all. She sighed and waited for the class to begin.

The professor continued. "We'll be honing our wish identification skills as we try to determine exactly what Mica is wishing for this morning." She clasped her hands together and smiled at the students. "I'll start with an easy question. Who can tell me what type of creature Mica is?"

Hands shot into the air. Cassie kept hers down. Too easy.

"Gloryah?" said the professor, pointing to a student with a pinkish-orange glow. Cassie liked her; she had a sweet disposition and was exceedingly polite, a trait Cassie admired greatly.

"A moonbug!" said Gloryah. But her brow wrinkled as the words came out of her mouth. "No, that's not right. I mean a—"

"It's a glowfur," interjected a student named Aerabelle disdainfully. She snorted. "Even my baby sister knows the difference between a glowfur and a moonbug!"

"I knew that!" Gloryah said. She looked around the room, appealing to her classmates. "I really did!"

Cassie gave Gloryah an understanding smile (though, really, who could mix those two up?) and turned to bestow a frown on Aerabelle, who had dusky purple curls and a deceptively sweet round face. You were not supposed to react negatively to your classmates; that was one of Starling Academy's basic rules. Being kind and supportive—no matter how silly you thought a comment or question was—helped create an atmosphere of civility and support, which encouraged sharing and open dialogue, per the Student Manual. Aerabelle had apparently skipped that chapter.

"Be kind, Aerabelle," the professor said in a warning voice. She might have been tiny, but her toughness was legendary. Her eyes flashed with annoyance. "That's what we are here for. To learn, of course, but to do so in a supportive way. There are no incorrect answers. We learn from everything that is shared in this classroom, accurate or inaccurate. There is no room for negativity here."

Aerabelle pouted, clearly not comprehending her teacher's words, just her scolding tone. Cassie wasn't surprised. The purple-haired girl was part of a group of first years whose ringleader was a student named Vivica, who had been particularly rude to the Star Darlings from day one at Starling Academy. Aerabelle was just as kind and understanding as her pale blue friend, Vivica—which is to say not at all.

Cassie watched as Gloryah's face burned brightly with embarrassment. Cassie felt sorry for the girl but was quick to notice that she flushed a very pretty shade. Whenever Cassie blushed, her cheeks turned a silvery shade that she thought was very unflattering.

Professor Lucretia Delphinus pointed to the glowfur, who gazed at the class serenely. "Class, please say hello to Mica," the professor instructed.

"Star greetings, Mica," said the class, and Mica rewarded them with a few notes from the "Song of Meeting New People." His singing was very pretty, though slightly muffled thanks to his bulging cheeks, stuffed with Green Globules. Cassie smiled. Glowfurs were notoriously greedy. The golden star on Mica's belly glowed in greeting.

The students all oohed and aahed, as you would do if you didn't have a pet glowfur who lived in your room and glowed its starbelly at you every morning. The creature blinked its large eyes at the students. A sigh went up.

"She's so cute!" Aerabelle cried.

"Actually, she's a he," corrected Cassie gently. But really, how could the girl not see that his belly star was half the size of a female's, the surest indicator?

"Whatever," said Aerabelle with a shrug.

Cassie shook her head. Some Starlings!

"So what is this glowfur wishing for?" the professor asked the class. "Concentrate and pay attention to the signals. This will be the most challenging part of your Wish Missions. Wishlings make many wishes, sometimes several a day. The key is to deduce their special wish."

The students all stared at the glowfur, who looked right back at them, his large eyes serious, his little paws buried in the fur on top of his head. *So that's it!* thought Cassie. His wish was suddenly so apparent to her it was like it was stamped on the middle of his furry little forehead. She felt a rush of positive energy flow through her.

Piece of pie, she thought, using a Wishworld expression her roommate had taught her. She looked around, waiting for someone to pick up on the obvious clue.

"He's hungry!" called out a girl named Tansy.

"Yes, that's it. Mica wants his breakfast!" a blue-tinged classmate chimed in.

"That's not it," said the professor. "Try again. When you figure it out, you may feel a burst of energy. But unfortunately, that doesn't happen for everyone."

Cassie yawned. With a quick glance to make sure that her professor's attention was focused elsewhere, she slipped her Star-Zap into her lap and flipped it open. She began composing a holo-text message to Vega and Scarlet.

 Do either of you have early lunch? We could meet up.

 Second lunch.

  No, last lunch. And I'm already hungry!

 Then meet after SD class? What a mess in the caf this morning, huh?

 That was crazy! Sounds good.

Okay with me.

 We have to figure out how to get our hands on those flowers! Any ideas?

 Vega?

 Scarlet?

 You two there?

 Hello?

Still no response. Cassie tried to keep an eye on her screen as well as on her teacher. She stole a glance at Mica, whose pink fur was now standing up on his head in his obvious irritation. She was about to raise her hand to reveal the wish and help put the glowfur out of his misery when her Star-Zap began to vibrate and beep loudly. She scrambled to silence it and dropped her Star-Zap on the floor. It landed with a loud clatter and slid to the middle of the classroom, out of her reach.

Starf! She thought she had put it in silent mode.

Her classmates stared at her, openmouthed. The room was so still you could have heard a glowfur gasp. With as much dignity as she could muster, she walked over to pick up her Star-Zap. The tiny professor glided over and held out her hand. Shamefaced, Cassie placed the Star-Zap in her palm.

"Star apologies," muttered Cassie. For a girl who hated to call attention to herself, this was an extraordinarily mortifying moment. She stood in front of her teacher, unsure what to do next.

"Outside," the professor said sternly, turning and heading toward the classroom door, which opened smoothly. As Cassie followed the teacher out of the room, she was well aware that all eyes, including Mica's, were on her.

To Cassie's dismay, the professor began to lecture her in front of the open doorway, in view of the entire class, which seemed to be hanging on every word. "Now, Cassie, I am very disappointed in you," the professor said sternly. "You know that there is no holo-texting allowed in the classroom. Your behavior was disrespectful and inexcusable."

Cassie shut her eyes. This was her worst nightmare. More than once she had dreamed of being humiliated in front of her class. And it was even more distressing and embarrassing than she had imagined it would be. *What is going to happen to me?* she wondered. *Will she keep my Star-Zap to teach me a lesson? Give me an extra holo-report assignment on wish identification? Or could it be something worse?* She had heard rumors of a double secret detention room for badly misbehaving students that featured uncomfortable chairs and a special light that masked everyone's glow, leaving them looking like dull Wishlings. She was sure it was a star legend that upperclassmen told to scare unsuspecting first years, but she certainly didn't want to find out.

She braced herself for the punishment that was no doubt to come. The classroom door slid shut behind her silently and ominously.

Cassie gulped.

CHAPTER

4

"**How was that?**" said the professor.

Cassie was confused. "Star-starscuse me?" she stammered. She looked up to see her that her teacher was grinning down at her.

"I was just putting on a show for the rest of the students," Professor Lucretia Delphinus explained, handing Cassie her Star-Zap. "You know, make them think I was really annoyed with you. I didn't want to blow your cover." She put a hand on Cassie's shoulder. "Pretty convincing, huh?"

Cassie nodded. She was still so tense she was unable to speak. Professor Lucretia Delphinus had been convincing, all right!

"Look, I realize how boring these introductory classes can be for you when your studies have already taken you so much further," the professor continued.

Cassie nodded again. Relief flowed over her and she was finally able to give the teacher a shaky smile.

"For the rest of these girls," Professor Lucretia Delphinus explained, "wish identification is something that will happen staryears from now. For you, it could happen any starmin."

Cassie felt her stomach give a little flip of anxiety. Professor Lucretia Delphinus's words brought her both extreme excitement and crippling terror. Each time another Star Darling was chosen to go on a mission, she could see the looks of disappointment on the other girls' faces and realized they did not experience the same over-whelming feeling of relief that swept through her.

Professor Lucretia Delphinus raised a finger as an idea came to her. "I know! I'm going to go inside and tell the rest of the class that I sent you to Lady Stella's office for a chat. That will keep them on their toes!" She laughed a conspiratorial laugh as she smoothed her skirt. "Why don't you go to the Luminous Library and relax until your next class?" She paused for a moment as if she was considering whether to say something else. "Cassie, maybe you could spend some time mulling over what's been bothering you."

Cassie looked at the teacher quizzically.

"You look like you have the weight of Starling Academy on your shoulders," the teacher explained. She looked deep into Cassie's eyes. "Is there anything you want to talk about?"

Cassie felt her chest expand for a moment when she thought of the possibility of having an adult ally. A grown-up to trust? An authority figure to share her worries with? It was like being presented with an unexpected but extremely valuable gift. But she couldn't get rid of the feeling that she just shouldn't trust anyone. She shook her head. "Actually, everything's fine," she fibbed. "I'm just worried about my Wish History assignment. Star salutations for understanding what happened in class. I'm really sorry."

The teacher nodded. "Now I'd better get back inside and help poor Mica," she said. "Of course, as you probably already figured out, he's wishing . . ."

"For a mirror so he can begin his daily grooming," finished Cassie. She could tell by the irritated way he had been preening his whiskers.

Her teacher smiled. "That he is, the vain little thing!"

★

The thought of having forty starmins to herself before her next class put a little bounce in Cassie's step. She walked down the hall, her footfalls echoing, as she considered her options. She could go to the Lightning Lounge and clear her mind in a meditation room and possibly come up with a clever idea for disposing of Astra and Clover's flowers. Since those two had had their flowers the longest, she thought that they could certainly put up a fight to keep them. She might have to do some fancy footwork. Or she could steal some time for herself and finish the last chapter of the holo-book she was reading. It was her uncle's latest thriller, which would definitely relax her. (It wasn't even available to the public yet, but she was certain it would be another runaway best seller.) She was pretty sure she had the mystery all figured out, but Uncle Andreas often threw a few misleading clues (also known as drifting moonbugs) into his stories, so she was really interested to find out if her hunch was correct. Not wanting to waste any of her free time, she sat on a nearby starmarble bench and pulled out her holo-book.

The words leapt into the air and she began to

read eagerly. Her uncle's books used IMT, the new Illuminated Manuscript Technology: anytime the reader wanted to see the action unfold, she just needed to push a button and the animated holo-scene would play, with the text read aloud as it happened. It was a thrilling way to experience a story, especially a mystery. She got to a particularly exciting passage and pressed the IMT button.

She held her breath as Detective Marmaduke Carbuncle stepped out of the shadowy recesses of a dark alley in Starland City. "Hold it right there, NT-96," he called.

"I . . . um . . . This does not compute!" Bot-Bot NT-96 barked. And suddenly it began to go berserk, ramming its metal body against the wall, sparks flying. Detective Carbuncle dove for cover as the Bot-Bot burst into—

"Um, starscuse me?" someone said meekly.

Cassie turned the book off with an irritated swipe. She turned to the figure that stood in front of her. "Yes?" she said through gritted teeth. There was nothing Cassie hated as much as being interrupted when she was reading.

"Um, hi, Cassie. Sorry for bothering you."

Cassie blinked. It was Ophelia. Her bright yellow hair hung on either side of her face in two pigtails. She wore a plain yellow T-shirt and a pair of overalls, which were a little short, so her yellow-and-white-striped socks peeked out. She was so tiny and frail that she made Cassie feel tall, an unfamiliar sensation for her. When she gazed down at the girl, she realized the height difference made her feel motherly and protective.

"Oh, hi," Cassie replied. "I was just talking about you with Leona."

The girl's wide ochre eyes filled with liquid-glitter tears. "Oh, Leona," she said. "I miss her so much. She was a wonderful roommate."

"Really?" said Cassie, who imagined that sharing a room with Leona would involve a large amount of appreciative observation. And applause.

"Oh, yes," she breathed. "She was so entertaining! Always putting on such fun shows. It was like going to the theater! Every day!"

"So where are you living now?" Cassie asked.

"I have a single room in the Little Dipper Dorm," said Ophelia sadly. "It's pretty lonely. I really miss Leona and also being a . . ." She looked around, saw that the hallway was deserted, and lowered her voice anyway. "A Star Darling."

Cassie nodded.

Ophelia leaned her head to one side, thinking. "I know I had some trouble fitting in. And my Wish Mission was a disaster, of course. But I really tried. Because I . . . I liked it. I finally felt like I belonged somewhere. Now I just feel kind of lost."

Cassie understood completely. "It was nice to belong to something special," she said. "Now you're just another Starling Academy student."

"That's right," said Ophelia. "That's exactly right."

"I understand you more than you know," said Cassie. She was starting to feel even more protective toward the girl. "I don't tell a lot of people about this, but I'm an orphan, too."

Ophelia gulped and looked away. "I'm sorry," she said. She let her eyes wander around the hallway, unable make eye contact with Cassie for a moment.

Cassie was touched. "Girls like us, we need to stick together," she said. She was overwhelmed with an unfamiliar desire to hug Ophelia and make her feel better. Let her know that she wasn't alone. She felt ashamed for the unkind thoughts she had had about the girl before.

"It's just so . . . hard here," said Ophelia.

Cassie nodded. "It *is* hard," she said. "It's so big and there's so much to learn and so many new people. It's difficult to be away from home. . . ." Her voice trailed off as she realized her slip. How thoughtless of her! Ophelia didn't have a home; what had she been thinking?

But Ophelia leaned forward eagerly. "I know!" she said. "My mom says . . ."

Cassie looked at the girl in sympathy. "I used to do the same thing right after my parents began their afterglow," she said. "It's hard to talk about someone you love so much in the past tense, since they're still so present for you."

"What?" said Ophelia. Her eyes widened and she shifted in place. "Oh, yeah," she said. "What I meant was that my mom *used* to tell me that you need to find a group of friends who make you sparkle. And I thought I found it with you Starlings."

"Just because you're not an official Star Darling, it doesn't mean we can't help to make you sparkle," Cassie told the girl gently.

Ophelia's face lit up. "Star salutations, Cassie," she said.

The bell rang and girls began to swarm out of their classrooms. Ophelia was jostled a bit. "I'll holo-text you later," said Cassie as she turned to head down the hallway toward her next class. "I'll see you again soon. Cross my stars and hope to shine," she promised.

Ophelia smiled wanly. "I'd like that," she said softly.

She then turned and merged into the current of students, her small yellow-pigtailed head disappearing almost immediately.

Cassie stared after her, a smile on her face. All Ophelia needed was some friends, poor thing. She started toward the science stellation for her next class, then stopped in her tracks.

"Watch it!" said a blue-haired girl. "First year!" she remarked to a friend.

A sudden thought crossed Cassie's mind. She knew why *she* was roaming the hallways during first period. But why hadn't Ophelia been in class?

CHAPTER
5

"I'm sorry," said Vega. "I never got your holo-text. Scarlet and I have band practice right now, anyway. We can't go with you."

Cassie smiled at Scarlet. Despite her disappointment, she was glad to hear that the girl was back in the band.

Most of the Star Darlings were standing in the Star Quad, the area in the middle of campus. Their secret S.D. lessons, the last class of the day, had just let out. The girls usually chatted outside a bit before they headed off to their respective clubs, sports, lessons, studies, and other leisure activities before dinnertime.

"What time will it be over?" Cassie asked. "Maybe we could do it afterwards?" She really didn't feel confident confronting the two roommates by herself.

"No, then I'm meeting Professor Elara Ursa to talk about an extra-credit assignment," Vega explained.

Cassie wanted to ask if that couldn't wait until the next starday, but she saw the determined look in Vega's eyes. She knew that Vega's dream was to be the top student at Starling Academy and that she would do whatever it took to get there. She turned to Scarlet.

"And I have an Intuition study group," offered Scarlet. "I've really got to go since I missed all those classes. Star apologies."

"So I have to go get the flowers alone?" Cassie asked.

"Can't it wait till tomorrow?" asked Vega.

Cassie glanced at Astra and Clover, who were arguing again. She gasped as Astra snatched the hat off Clover's head and tossed it into the air, levitating it with wish energy in a cruel game of keep-away.

"I guess you're right," said Vega. "The sooner, the better."

"And this is the only afternoon Astra has off from practice this week," Cassie explained. "I overheard her saying she was going back to her room to watch old holo-vids of the team they are playing on Bopday."

Vega considered this. "You'll have to convince only her," she said. "Clover will be at band practice with us."

"That's a plus," said Cassie, her mood lightening a bit.

"So what's your plan?" Scarlet asked.

"Oh, look!" shouted someone. Cassie turned around and gasped. The nimble Clover had scrambled up the trunk of a nearby ballum-blossom tree and now stood on a sturdy branch, her arms held out to the sides. She didn't hesitate for even a moment before walking its length like a tightrope. Clover paused for a starsec, then leapt off, plucking the hat out of the air. She landed neatly, not a hair out of place. With a smirk at Astra, who looked like she was fuming, Clover jauntily placed the hat on her head and gave a deep bow. The rest of the Star Darlings applauded.

Vega shook her head. "I keep forgetting that she's one of the Flying Molensas," she said, referring to the most well-known circus family on Starland. "That girl is a born acrobat!"

"Impressive," Cassie said, turning back to Vega and Scarlet.

"So, your plan?" Vega prompted her.

"Right," said Cassie. "My plan is . . ." She sighed. "Actually, my plan is to come up with a plan on my way to their room."

Scarlet snorted.

Vega sucked in her cheeks. "Not much of a plan," she said.

"You're telling me," Cassie replied.

"Well, good luck with that!" Vega said, grimacing. "If it doesn't happen, we can always try again tomorrow."

Scarlet nodded. "I'm free."

"Star salutations," replied Cassie. She was determined to put an end to the nonsense that day.

She watched as the two girls headed to the Lightning Lounge with Sage, Leona, and Libby. That was good. Sure, Scarlet was straggling behind, keeping apart from everyone, but she was getting back into the swing of things and that was what mattered.

Cassie turned around, looking for Astra, but she had already left. Cassie hopped on the Cosmic Transporter, hoping that the girl had gone straight back to her room. The flower business needed to end that day. She had a bigger dish to dry. She grinned as she recalled another Wishling expression one of the Star Darlings had shared with her. *I'm going to knock their clocks off when it's my turn to go down to Wishworld*, she thought. Her words were brave but her stomach flipped at the very thought.

★

Cassie took a deep breath and knocked on Astra and Clover's door. Her mind was a complete blank and she noticed that her hands were trembling a bit out of sheer nervousness. She pulled a piece of boingtree gum out of her pocket. She found its mellow taste soothed her nerves. Then she unwrapped another for good measure and shoved it into her mouth. A vanishing garbage can stood nearby and Cassie tossed her wrappers into it. She wondered how she was going to connect with Astra. The Starling was a total sports fanatic and Cassie didn't know a star ball from a star . . . a star something.

She was chomping away, still hoping for some stellar inspiration, when the door slid open. Cassie's head snapped up. Astra stood there, a star ball tucked under her arm.

"Cassie!" said Astra. "I have the star ball game on. But I thought I heard something."

"Um, do you mind if I come in?"

"Of course not," said Astra, stepping aside. She slid the door closed behind them.

Cassie was so keyed up she was practically vibrating with nervous energy. She was certain that Astra would notice and get suspicious. But the girl turned back to her star ball game without another glance. Cassie looked around the room, which was both sporty and sleek, reflecting the personalities of the two roommates. It was her first visit to their room, and her eyes took in Astra's side, with its star ball court and shelves lined with sporting equipment and startrophies of all shapes and sizes. The star ball game Astra was watching was playing on a screen that took up an entire wall. Clover's side had an extra-high ceiling and was filled with musical instruments and some technical-looking machines. Cassie noted with interest a terrarium, lush and green, built right into the floor.

"That's Stellar School playing Comet Prep a couple of weeks ago," said Astra, her eyes never leaving the screen. "We're playing Stellar on Bopday. They're really good, so I'm watching a holo-vid of their last couple of games to get some pointers on how to approach the game."

Cassie nodded. Sounded good.

"Just let me watch this last play and I'm all yours," said Astra.

"VALENCIA DODGES THE ONCOMING CENTER AND PIVOTS. SHE JUMPS! SHE SHOOTS! SHE SCORES!" the announcer shouted. The crowd went wild. Astra turned back to Cassie. "This game is over," she said, even though Comet Prep now had the ball. "It's all over but the sparkling."

"Oh," said Cassie, not understanding.

"There's not enough time left for them to tie," Astra explained. "So how can I help you?" she asked, cradling the star ball in the crook of her arm as if it was a baby.

Cassie wandered to the vase of glittery flowers, which never faded or lost their bloom, sitting on a table right between the two girls' sides of the room. She thought she'd try the direct approach one more time. "You know we all got these flowers, right?" she began.

Astra nodded distractedly.

"Well, Vega and I took one of the bouquets to the botany lab and found out that they are full of negative energy. Like off the charts. They were grown on the Isle of Misera. Everyone has gotten rid of their flowers but you. We think they are causing you and Clover to fight all the time." She paused to gauge Astra's reaction.

"That's ridiculous," Astra laughed. "They're so beautiful. And they smell so amazing. Like florafierces." She laughed again. "Though that crazy roommate of mine thinks they smell just like purple piphanies."

Cassie sighed. The flowers had worked their intoxicating magic on Astra. She had to come up with another plan. She had come to realize that these strange flowers smelled different to everyone. For example, she could only smell the strong odor of silverbellas. She figured that the blooms, perhaps to entice you into not discarding them, gave off the smell of your own favorite flower. And she also knew from experience that it was impossible to convey that to someone who hadn't figured it out on her own. The silverbella odor was actually so strong to Cassie that it was overwhelming and very distracting. She found herself wanting to lean over and bury her nose in the blossoms. She countered this by taking a step back and concentrating on breathing only through her mouth.

Suddenly, she had a startacular idea. Okay, maybe it was a startacularly crazy idea. She'd find out soon enough.

"I just read this amazing holo-article about keeping flowers in your room," she fibbed. "It involves sports, so I thought you'd want to be the first to know."

"Really?" said Astra, leaning forward. She knew that Cassie read more than all the other Star Darlings put together, so it was perfectly reasonable that she would have seen a holo-article Astra had missed.

"Three . . . two . . . one," the announcer counted down, and a buzzer went off. "STELLAR SCHOOL WINS AGAIN! AND THE CROWD GOES WILD!"

Astra lowered the volume with a wave of her hand and turned toward Cassie with interest. Behind her, Cassie could see the players jumping up and down, huge grins on their faces, but she tried not to let it distract her from her mission.

"Well, the holo-article said that athletes should avoid having fresh flowers in their room before a big event," Cassie said. "Apparently, it weakens their powers of concentration."

Astra stared at her. "Really?" she said. She gave the flowers a quizzical look. "That's terrible! And here I have that big game coming up."

Cassie nodded sympathetically, biting her lip.

Astra tossed the star ball onto a chair and picked up the vase of flowers. With a confused expression on her face, she held them out to Cassie, whose heart skipped a beat. *Is my crazy idea actually going to work?* she thought.

Suddenly, Astra closed her eyes and brought the flowers to her nose. She took a deep sniff and her face grew serious. "I don't know," she said, hugging the flowers to her chest. "They just smell so good. . . ."

Cassie stole a glance at the wall and spotted a holo-poster of a sporty-looking woman with her name emblazoned underneath. She winked at Cassie, as if in encouragement. Cassie hated to lie; in fact, it pained her to do so. *But this is for Astra and Clover's own good*, she thought. *They'll be grateful when the flowers are gone and things can go back to normal.*

She took a deep breath and spoke. "Um, as a matter of fact, they interviewed a top athlete named Saturnia, who said as soon as she threw out a bouquet of flowers she had in her house, she felt so much better."

"Really?" said Astra, her eyes narrowing. "And they interviewed her recently?"

Cassie nodded. "Just this morning," she said. "This news is hot off the holo-presses."

"Aha!" Astra said with a laugh as she put down the flowers (but not before taking another long, deep sniff). "Good joke, Cassie!" she said. "You had me going until you brought up Saturnia. She's in training for the Starlympics and she's in a remote mountain location. She won't be giving any interviews for starmonths."

Oh, starf! thought Cassie. "Ha-ha, I almost got you!" she said weakly. "Good joke, huh?" Her heart sank. What was she going to do now? She had to come up with something—and quick. She scanned the room, looking for something—anything—that would give her some inspiration. Her eyes fell on a stick with a star-shaped net on its end propped up in the corner, and she picked it up. "The real reason I came over was to ask you for help. Believe it or not, I'm not doing very well in P.E."

"Physical Energy?" asked Astra, a shocked look on her face.

"Yes, Physical Energy," said Cassie. "I was wondering if you could teach me how to handle this star . . ." Her mind raced. What was that thing called, anyway?

"Starstick," said Astra. "It's called a starstick. You know, for playing Star-Away. It's an important skill to master. You've come to the right place." She raced to a closet, threw open the door, and started tossing sports equipment behind her. "There it is," she said, pulling out another starstick and a medium-sized ball. She tossed the ball into the net at the end of her stick and began to bounce it up and down. "You know, where you have to get the ball into your opponent's basket to score a point? It's a lot of fun."

"Riiiight," said Cassie, nodding. All these star sports were so similar to her she could never keep them straight.

After showing Cassie how to hold the starstick properly, Astra tossed her the ball. But Cassie's initial instinct was to duck. The ball hit the wall and bounced to the floor.

Astra shook her head. "You're supposed to *catch* it, silly," she explained. "Hand me the ball." Cassie did and Astra placed it in her net and tried again. That time Cassie bobbled the ball for a moment but held on to it.

"Great job!" said Astra encouragingly. "Now toss it back to me."

Cassie did. Her throw was off target and Astra had to lunge sideways. Still, she caught it neatly.

Toss after toss, Cassie began to fall into the rhythm. Scoop and toss, scoop and toss. "Hey, this is kind of fun!" she said.

"It is," Astra agreed. "Just wait till you try star ball," she added.

Cassie could see the flowers out of the corner of her eye, mocking her with their mere existence, their presence intensified by the cloying smell of silverbellas. Suddenly, she had another crazy idea. She had no idea if it would work. But she kept moving closer and closer to the vase of flowers. The two girls tossed the ball back and forth, back and forth as she made her way across the room.

She was within arm's reach of the blooms. And suddenly, the front door slid open. Clover was standing there. Cassie saw her chance. She tossed the ball as far past Astra as she could, then scooped up the vase of flowers in the net of her starstick.

Astra jumped over her round red couch and made a flying leap, catching the ball.

"Duck!" Cassie cried to Clover. Looking puzzled, Clover did. And Cassie hurled the vase of flowers as hard as she could. Astra turned around, obviously pleased with her stellar catch. When she saw her beloved flowers hurtling through the air toward the open door, her mouth opened in shock. It seemed to Cassie as if everything was happening in slow motion: Astra's loud "Noooooo!" and her desperate lunge for the flowers. But she was too late, for miraculously, Cassie's aim was true. The flowers landed right inside the mouth of the waiting disappearing garbage can and then they were gone—instantly.

Cassie was panting hard as Clover straightened up. The roommates were both staring at Cassie in shocked silence. Astra scowled at her. "Cassie!" she shouted. "Why in the stars did you . . ." Then she noticed her roommate. "Clover!" she said pleasantly. "There you are! How did band practice go?"

"It was great," said Clover. "Star salutations for asking. Did you have a fun time with Cassie?"

"I did," said Astra. "Who knew Cassie was such a natural Star-Away player? Did you see that throw? I'm going to tell the coach we've got a brand-new hurler!"

And Cassie began to laugh. The last of the flowers were gone. Sure, she was still worried. There was still the question of who had sent them—and why. But she laughed anyway—with relief that the flowers were finally gone, with happiness that the roommates were back to normal, and also with pleasure that she had actually discovered a sport she enjoyed!

CHAPTER
6

 Operation: Flower Disposal a success! The S.D. are now flower-free. Let's meet after dinner to talk about next steps!

 Vega?

 Scarlet?

No answer. Again. This was getting weird. Something must be wrong with the Star-Zaps' holo-connections, Cassie decided. There were a lot of missed messages lately. Cassie's stomach rumbled. She had worked up quite an appetite playing starstickball—or whatever it was called. She checked her Star-Zap. It wasn't quite dinnertime, but she didn't feel like being in her room any longer. She decided to take a stroll in the ozziefruit orchard before dinner.

★

Cassie meandered through the trees, which were heavy with fruit. The smell of ripe ozziefruit was mouth-watering. Flutterfocuses wafted among the trees, and glimmerbees darted about, on a mission. She took a seat on a low stone wall and closed her eyes, enjoying the slight breeze and the gentle warmth of the late-afternoon sun on her upturned face.

"Cassie! What a nice starprise!" said someone with a familiar voice.

Cassie's eyes snapped open. A shadowy figure stood in front of her, blocking the sun. She squinted, but it wasn't until she shielded her eyes that she could see who it was. She gave an involuntary gasp.

"Lady Stella!" she said. "What are you doing here?"

Lady Stella laughed. "Just enjoying a pre-dinner stroll through the ozziefruit orchard, same as you," she answered. She motioned her head toward the stone wall. "Mind if I join you?" she asked.

"Not at all," said Cassie. She sat up straight and smoothed her skirt. She hadn't been alone with the headmistress since the day of her Starling Academy interview, many starmonths earlier. Truth be told, she found the headmistress, as lovely and kind as she was, a little intimidating.

Lady Stella smiled and sat down next to her. "I love the light this time of day," she said. "It's not as stunning as lightfall, but it has its own stark beauty. Everything looks so sharp and focused, you know?"

Cassie nodded. She did know. She felt the same way.

"And it's the perfect time to come to the orchards. Most people are getting ready for dinner, so you have them all to yourself."

Cassie nodded again. "Yes," she managed to say in agreement. She felt tongue-tied around the headmistress. She yearned to say something intelligent and thoughtful, but couldn't think of anything at the moment. Her face became warm and she knew that her cheeks were turning that unflattering shade of silver she so disliked.

"May I be frank with you, Cassie?" Lady Stella asked.

Cassie nodded nervously.

"You've been on my mind recently."

Cassie gulped. She had?

"I've been wanting to ask you a question. Why do you think you are here at Starling Academy? Why do you think you were chosen to be a Star Darling?"

Cassie took off her glasses and peered through them to grab a starmin to think. She had an idea, but she felt nervous about saying it aloud. She didn't want to seem like a braggart. So she shrugged.

"I only ask because you don't seem as confident as you should be. Take it from me, Cassie. You know that you and your fellow Star Darlings were chosen for your strengths, and what you bring to the group, each something different. You are one of the most intuitive students I have ever come across in my career. You scored off the charts on the entrance exams." Lady Stella gave her a sympathetic look. "You must learn to recognize your strengths and trust yourself."

"St-star salutations," said Cassie. She was both happy to have her suspicions confirmed and disappointed that she hadn't spoken up for herself. It was an odd mix of emotions.

Lady Stella stood and turned to go, then turned back. "I know you are dreading your mission, Cassie," she said. "I'd be a fool not to see it. But I am telling you that you have nothing to fear. You're going to be a natural."

"Star salutations, Lady Stella," Cassie repeated. She watched the headmistress's retreating back. Again she felt a rush of different feelings—embarrassment at being so transparent, relief that Lady Stella had faith in her, and hope that she would be successful when her mission actually happened. With a sigh, she headed to the Celestial Café for dinner. On her way, she thought she heard a rustling in the branches behind her. She turned around sharply, but no one was there.

When she walked into the bustling cafeteria and made her way to the Star Darlings' table, she was struck by the sinking sun, which lit up the sky with its warm rosy tones. She knew that as soon as the beams hit the Crystal Mountains, the view would be even more spectacular, as prisms of rainbow light would begin to appear. But what really caught her attention was the fact that Astra and Clover were sitting side by side, looking quite chummy. As Cassie pulled out a chair and sat down, she saw the Bot-Bot waiter from that starmorning zoom up with the roommates' drinks. He hesitated for a moment before placing them on the table.

Clover threw her arms up in front of Astra. "Don't worry SL-D9," she cried. "I've got you covered!" The two girls cracked up.

"Star salutations," said the Bot-Bot sincerely as he carefully placed the drinks out of Astra's reach.

Vega raised her eyebrows at Cassie, who nodded.

Vega gave her a triple wink, the Starlandian way of silently telling someone "Good job!"

Scarlet came in and sat down next to Cassie. "All good?" she asked quietly.

Across the table, Clover laughed out loud. "Oh, Astra, you're so funny!" she said.

Cassie grinned. "All good," she said.

Dinner, for the first time in more than a double starweek, was extremely pleasant—argument- and drama-free. The girls talked and laughed and joked and traded bites of their dishes. Even Leona and Scarlet seemed to be getting along, or at least not fighting with each other, which was good enough in Cassie's holo-book. Cassie had a huge smile on her face for the entire meal.

The Bot-Bot waiter came over to take their dessert order.

Tessa ordered first, as usual. "I'll have an ozziefruit parfait and a mug of hot—" she began. Just then, their Star-Zaps chimed, all twelve at the same time. It made a pleasant, musical sound to Cassie's ears.

Adora read the holo-text first. "Starmendous!" she said. She looked up. "Hey, everybody, listen to this! We're invited to a party!"

The table started to buzz. A party! How fun! *It's just*

what we all need, thought Cassie. *A chance to relax and just enjoy ourselves for a couple of hours.* All the girls flipped open their Star-Zaps as the Bot-Bot waiter hovered nearby, forgotten. Gemma read the invitation out loud. " 'You are invited to a Star Mani/Pedi Party tonight after dinner in the Lightning Lounge's party room. Hydrongs of polish colors to choose from, state-of-the-art star-beautychambers, music, dancing, a floating dessert bar . . .' " She paused. "What's a floating dessert bar? We don't have those in Solar Springs."

Libby, who lived in a mansion and had been to too many fancy parties to count, supplied the answer. "Oh, you'll love it! It's a levitating cloudcandy table covered with every light-as-air dessert you've ever heard of," she said. "You know—Aeropuffs, Floating Wisps, Featherwhispers. They're so startastically delicious they just melt in your mouth. There are cocomoon star-pillows and . . ."

"Say no more. I'm in," said Tessa. She canceled her dessert order and stood up. The rest of the girls followed suit.

On her way out the door, Cassie spotted Ophelia sitting alone at a table, idly twirling a noddlenoodle on her fork and staring into space.

"I hope it's not too crowded," said Vega worriedly as they approached the Lightning Lounge. But when they pushed open the doors to the party room, they discovered they were the first to arrive.

"Oh, my stars!" said Sage, taking in the shifting, shimmering multicolored stars that were projected on the walls, floor, and ceiling; the multileveled dance floor; the colorful starbeautychambers, round and shiny; and the floating dessert bar, which was even better than it sounded, with edible fluffy pastel pink, blue, and yellow clouds of spun sugar candy suspended in the air. Nestled in the candyfloss were sweet little confections in all the colors of the rainbow. Tessa made a glitter-beeline for the sweets and loaded up a sparkling crystal plate with some carefully selected treats. The rest of the girls did the same. After eating three jujufruit gossamer-wisps, which, she was pleased to discover, were as light and airy as they were delicious, Cassie's mind returned to Ophelia, who'd been sitting all by herself in the cafeteria. She flipped open her Star-Zap and started typing.

 Ophelia, we're all at the Lightning Lounge, at a mani/pedi party. The desserts are out of this world! Come join us!

That sounds startacular! I'll be right over!

We're downstairs in the party room. See you soon!

Cassie smiled as she shut her Star-Zap. Her good deed for the day was done. Now she was ready for some beauty time.

"I don't know why the rest of the students aren't here," said Adora as she reached up to grab a hunk of pale blue spun sugar candy, as fluffy as a cloud. "But that just means more dessert for us!"

Cassie walked across the room and hesitated in front of a silvery chamber, unsure what to do next. Libby appeared at her side. "Let me help you," she said. "My mom has one," she explained. "Starbeautychambers can give you manicures, pedicures, haircuts and styles, facials, body scrubs, face sparklings, you name it." She pressed a round button on the side and the chamber opened like a flower, revealing a holo-screen, a fluffy white seat, and four covered pods. "That's where you put your hands and feet," she explained. Cassie took off her silver slippers and lowered herself onto the cozy-looking seat. She gasped at how luxuriously soft it was.

Libby nodded. "Amazing, right?"

The holo-screen slid into place at lap level. The shape of a hand appeared on the screen, and Cassie hovered her palm over it, looking to Libby for confirmation. Libby nodded. "Put your hand right on it," she said encouragingly. Cassie obliged and a list of nail polish colors in her signature shade appeared on the right-hand side of the screen. When she touched the name of the polish with her free hand, an image of the color was projected on her nails so she could make a well-informed decision. Cassie considered them all. Silver Streak was pretty-ish; Icicle a bit too frosty; Sassy Sparkles not quite as tasteful as she'd like; Time of Shadows White too austere; and Storm Queen a little too gray. She thought she'd love Pink Snowflake but was just lukewarm about it. Finally, Magic and Moonbeams came up. She gasped with delight. It was pure perfection. Sparkly, iridescent, and silvery white, it glowed with the promise of stardust and enchantment. She chose it for both her fingers and toes and slipped her hands and feet inside the pods. They were immediately enveloped in warm lotion that smelled just like glimmerdrop cookies. Cassie closed her eyes and a scene came flooding back: a day she had come home from school to find her mom, her cheeks flushed and her silvery hair escaping from her bun and framing her face. She had been baking all day and presented Cassie with a plate of warm cookies, which Cassie munched as she told her mom all about her day. It brought a sweet smile to her face and Cassie pressed the memory function on her Star-Zap to record it so she'd be able to watch it on-screen whenever she liked. A Bot-Bot masseuse zoomed up and began to knead her shoulders, which were slightly achy from the vigorous game of Star-Away she had played earlier. Ah, that was heavenly. Her chamber began to softly play "Brighter Than a Comet," one of her favorite songs, and she hummed along. Once her hands and feet were sufficiently moisturized, they were massaged. Then the nails were trimmed and shaped, and finally the polish was applied.

Vega, who had gone back to the floating dessert bar for seconds, was on her way to get her own mani/pedi. She scanned the room and leaned over Cassie's chamber to talk to her privately. "If the whole school was invited, why are there only twelve chambers?" she asked. "That's not even close to enough."

That's a good question, Cassie thought, but then the pods released her hands and feet and she saw her fingers and toes, polished to a silvery perfection. "Oh," she breathed. "I picked the most perfect color ever."

Vega shrugged and headed to a shiny blue starbeauty-chamber.

"Cassie, let me see," called Adora from a sky-blue starbeautychamber nearby.

Cassie stood and walked to her. She considered putting her shoes back on but didn't want to cover up her sparkling toes. Adora leaned over to take a look. "Pretty," she said. A Bot-Bot masseuse was giving her a neck massage as she picked her polish color. "I can't decide between Cerulean Circus for my fingers," she said, clicking on it, "or Starbeam Dream." She looked up to Cassie for help. "Oh . . . um," said Cassie. They looked exactly the same to her. "Definitely Starbeam Dream," she finally said.

"You're right," said Adora. "It's much prettier." She didn't seem to need any help choosing Indigo Spell for her toes.

When everyone's nails were done, the girls reclined on overstuffed couches and admired each other's fingers and toes as they sipped tall sparkling drinks brought to them by hovering Bot-Bot waiters. Then the lights dimmed. The starlight show began to flash faster and the music got louder. Cassie was pleased to note that Leona was the first to jump up and begin to dance—barefoot, of course. Her fingers and toes sparkled in the dim light; she had chosen a polish that made her nails look as if they had been dipped in liquid gold, which Cassie took as another sign that she was improving. Leona crooked her finger, beckoning to Cassie, who began to shake her head, her usual self-conscious response. But the idea of everyone's eyes on her as she moved to the beat, which usually unnerved her, suddenly seemed like an appealing one. She jumped up and bopped over to Leona, who grinned and grabbed her hands. The two began to spin around and around, then broke apart and twirled in the empty space. Cassie closed her eyes and moved to the music, freely and joyously. She didn't worry that she looked silly, and she didn't care what anyone was thinking of her. All she knew was that she felt beautiful, and fluid, and natural—and like she never wanted to stop moving to the music. After a few minutes, the rest of the girls joined in. They were a jumping, twirling, grinning mass. They danced until they couldn't dance anymore, then flopped onto the couches in happy exhaustion.

Cassie closed her eyes, breathing hard. She opened her eyes to see Sage leaning over her. She was still laughing.

"Cassie, get up, it's time for bed," she said.

"All right, all right." Cassie swung her feet to the floor and reluctantly slipped on her shoes. With a sigh, she stood up. She admired her fingernails again under the flashing lights. "Wow," Cassie said. "I really picked the best color."

Adora grabbed her arm. "I thought you liked Starbeam Dream," she said almost inaudibly.

"The music's too loud," said Cassie. "What did you say?"

"I said, I thought you liked Starbeam Dream."

Cassie shrugged. "Glad you like it, too," she said. She looked at Vega. "Are you coming with us?" she asked.

"You should go, you shouldn't wait," Vega said, pointing to Piper, who was sipping a sea-green beverage through a straw. "I will wait for my roommate."

Cassie was sleepy. "Okay, I'll see you all in the . . ."

"Morning," finished Piper.

Clover stood and threw her arms around Cassie.

"See you at breakfast, Clover," Cassie said.

"Wait for me," said Leona. But then she never got up, so Cassie and Sage shrugged and headed back to their room. They chatted and giggled all the way back to the dorm. Cassie tumbled into bed, fully intending to get up in a starsec to use her toothlight and sparkle her face, but she found she was so tired she couldn't move. She couldn't even muster the energy to ask Sage to please quiet down. The girl was still giggling.

Weird, she thought. *Ophelia never showed up at the party. Something better must have come up. Maybe she's not as lonely as Leona thinks she is.*

Sage rolled over, trying, and failing, to muffle a laugh.

I am so much better at falling asleep than Sage, Cassie thought. And she was right. She drifted off to sleep.

CHAPTER
7

When Cassie awoke the next morning, she felt starmendous—so much so that she said it out loud. "I feel starmendous," she said. No, that wasn't quite right. "I *am* starmendous," she tried. Yes, that was much better.

She stepped out of bed and stubbed her toe. "Moons and stars!" she cried. "That hurt!"

She looked to her roommate, whose head was resting on her lavender pillowcase, for sympathy. Sage looked back at her and giggled.

"Sage!" said Cassie with a scowl. "I hurt myself!"

"I know," said Sage, trying to make a sad face and failing miserably. "But something about it is pretty funny."

"No," said Cassie earnestly. "It's actually not."

But apparently that was very amusing to Sage, too.

With as much dignity as she could muster, Cassie hobbled her way to the sparkle shower room. Even though her toe was throbbing, she couldn't help admiring herself in the mirror, her gossamer silvery-pink hair looking so, well, gossamery and lovely around her pale face.

★

Cassie stood on the Cosmic Transporter, on her way to breakfast, staring into space. Suddenly, she was startled by someone skipping by, almost knocking her over. She peered after her. *Was that Scarlet?* she wondered.

When Cassie arrived in the cafeteria, she found Scarlet and Piper already sitting at the table. Piper's amazingly long seafoam green hair was pulled back into a rippling ponytail. Cassie chose the seat next to her. "Good . . ." she started.

"Morning," Piper said pleasantly.

Leona and Adora arrived next. "I'm not hungry," Leona said. "I ran into Ophelia this morning and she gave me this delicious zoomberry turnover from the huge care package she just got. So I'm just going to get a cup of hot . . ."

"Zing," said Piper.

Leona gave her a funny look. "Ozziefruit tea," she said, correcting her.

Vega arrived next and sat on the other side of Cassie. She was followed by Astra and Clover, who sat on the other side of the table.

"Last night was so much fun," said Clover.

Vega nodded. "We did our nails, had snacks, and more."

Clover nodded. "Yes, we did!"

"It certainly was not a bore," Vega finished.

The Bot-Bot waiter arrived and began to take their breakfast orders. Cassie ordered a bowl of druderwomp flakes with starberries.

Moons and stars, that was a good order, Cassie thought. She addressed Adora, who sat across from her. "I hope you don't have breakfast envy!"

"I think I'll like mine better," said Adora.

"Starscuse me?" said Cassie.

"I think I'll like mine better," repeated Adora.

"Um . . . what?" said Cassie.

"I said I think I'll like mine better," Adora said patiently.

"Uh . . . that's great," said Cassie, who still couldn't understand what the girl was saying but was too embarrassed to ask her to repeat it a third time.

When it was Leona's turn, she thought for a moment

and ordered starcakes and tinsel toast with a slice of mooncheese.

Sage giggled. "I thought you said you weren't hungry!"

"What are you talking about?" said Leona.

Breakfast arrived in record time. Tessa took a bite, then got a confused look on her face. "Starscuse me," she said politely to the Bot-Bot, "but I asked for starberry waffles. These are moonberry."

"Star apologies," said the Bot-Bot waiter. "That is highly irregular. I'll fix that right away." He zoomed back to the kitchen and returned a few starmins later.

Tessa dug in to her new breakfast excitedly, took a bite, then shook her head. "Moonberries again!" she exclaimed. "How . . ."

"Delightful," finished Piper.

"No, how odd," she said.

"I hate moonberries," said Sage disgustedly. But she punctuated her statement with a delighted laugh.

Sage's giggle is really annoying, thought Cassie. *It would be so much less annoying if she had a sweet, tinkling laugh. Kind of like* . . . She thought for a minute. *Kind of like mine,* she decided. She practiced it, putting her hand over her mouth and tittering. She nodded. It was musical and quite pleasant.

Cassie's day went on starmendously. She felt emboldened enough to raise her hand in every class, even when she wasn't quite sure of the answer. And when every eye in the class was focused on her, somehow it didn't feel intimidating at all. *That was some pep talk Lady Stella gave me yestarday*, she thought.

At the end of the day it was time for their Star Darlings lessons. Cassie settled into her usual seat in the soundproof classroom. She was starprised to see a new, unfamiliar teacher in front of the room. She was one of the youngest teachers Cassie had ever seen, with super-short magenta hair that stuck up from her head in tiny spikes. She wore swirly leggings in shades of pink, red, and orange, a fitted jacket (which the Star Darlings would soon discover, as the class went on, changed color every ten starmins), and shiny orange boots.

"Hello, class," she said, standing and walking up and down the aisles as she spoke. "I am Kiri Lillibelle and I am thrilled to be your guest lecturer today. You may not know me, but I am certainly familiar with each and every one of you. I am the researcher who hand-selects all of your—"

"Outfits," offered Piper.

Kiri gave her a quizzical look. "No, Mirror Mantras," she said. "A Mirror Mantra is a very important part of a successful Wish Mission. By repeating your Mirror Mantra while gazing into a mirror, you will receive strength and centeredness. When you recite it together with your Wisher down on Wishworld, you can bring clarity and focus to her that will aid in wish fulfillment."

She began to walk around the room as she spoke. "Mirror Mantras used to be presented to Starling Academy students upon graduation. We had four star-years to determine the perfect message for each student. The timing was a little tighter for you Star Darlings," she said with a laugh. "But we were able to determine the correct mantras for each of you."

"How do you choose them?" asked Libby with a yawn.

"An excellent question," said Kiri. "They were carefully selected based on each of your personalities, strengths, and challenges."

"Challenges?" asked Astra.

"Yes, challenges," said Kiri. "It is not just your strengths that make you the special person you are, but also your challenges and how you face them."

"But we already know our mantras," said Leona. "They were assigned to us as soon as we found out we were Star Darlings."

"Yes," said Kiri patiently. "But we've determined that the more you use them before your Wish Mission, the more their strength will increase. We want you to become as familiar with your mantra as you are with your own name. We want to make sure that they become second nature to you, and that you use them to their fullest potential. We want you to know your mantras forwards and backwards."

The girls nodded.

"So let's begin!" The classroom door opened and a bevy of Bot-Bot assistants flew into the room, each holding a floating holo-mirror, which it placed in front of a student. Cassie gazed at herself and found herself taking off her starglasses to get a closer look at her eyelashes. They were so thick and lush! How had she never noticed them before? They were pretty starmazing, actually. She was about to lean over and ask Leona if she had noticed her lashes before—and, if so, why she had never called them to Cassie's attention—when Kiri began to speak again.

"Okay," she said. "Now let's go around the room and recite your mantras for each other. Why don't you start?" she asked, pointing to Sage, who sat in the front of the room.

Sage giggled nervously and cleared her throat. She gazed into the mirror levelly. "I believe in you," she said. "Glow for it!"

Even from the back of the room, Cassie could see that Sage's reflection took on a brilliant glow.

"Look at her reflection!" Kiri cried to the class. "Her glow is intensifying even here on Starland! This is some pretty powerful stuff!"

She turned back to Sage. "Okay," said Kiri. "How did that make you feel?"

"I felt really energized," Sage said with a laugh. "While I definitely felt the power of the mantra when I used it on Wishworld, I felt something extra just now. Maybe my mantra has even more power than I realized."

Kiri nodded enthusiastically. "That's exactly it. We're thinking that we have not yet taken full advantage of the power of the mantras. And we think that you as Star Darlings may have even greater mantra powers than the other students."

The room began to buzz with excitement. When they quieted down, Kiri went around the room and had the rest of the Star Darlings recite their mantras, one by one.

"It's all in the balance. Glimmer and shine!" said Libby, her pink ponytail shimmering.

Leona said: "You are a star. Light up the world!"

Scarlet reached into her back pocket for her drumsticks and beat out a drumroll on top of her desk before stating: "Abracadabra—time for some star power!" And even she looked impressed by the burst of sparkle in her reflection.

"Dreams can come true," said Piper when it was her turn. "It's your time to shine!"

"Stronger you make challenges," said Astra with a wide grin. "Glowin' get to time!"

"Huh?" said Kiri.

Astra blinked at Kiri innocently. "I thought you said you wanted us to know our mantras forwards and backwards!"

Kiri shook her head and moved on to the next Star Darling.

"Let your heart lead the way," Tessa said, smiling at her reflection.

Her little sister went next. "Make up your mind to blaze like a comet!" Gemma shouted.

Clover adjusted her purple hat and said, "Keep the beat and shine like the star you are!"

Hmmm, thought Cassie. *That's not a bad mantra at all. Maybe Clover got mine by mistake?* She hesitated. She knew that Kiri was waiting for her to speak, but for some reason she just didn't want to say her mantra out loud. She had gladly accepted it when she had first received it, but it suddenly didn't seem right to her at all.

Kiri smiled at her encouragingly. "Come on, Cassie, let's hear it," she said.

Cassie sighed. "Listen to your feelings. Let your inner light sparkle," she said in a monotone. She was surprised to see that her reflection got extra sparkly even though her heart wasn't in it.

"What's wrong, Cassie?" Kiri asked. "That's a lovely mantra, if I do say so myself."

Cassie shrugged. Suddenly, she had an idea—a brilliant one, in fact. "Do you ever change people's mantras?" she asked.

Kiri was clearly taken aback. "Are you pulling my leg?" she said.

Gemma stood up to take a look. "No, she isn't," she told Kiri seriously. "She's not even touching you!"

Astra snorted. "Good one, Gemma!"

"I was thinking of something a little more star-forward," said Cassie slowly.

"Star-forward?" asked the teacher, her brow wrinkled.

"You know," said Cassie. "Exciting. Vibrant. Like 'You are totally startacular.' Or maybe 'You are star-mendously talented,'" she suggested.

Kiri was frowning as she studied Cassie. "But the Mirror Mantras are carefully chosen to reflect each student's personality," she said. "A lot of work went into each one. I don't think I've ever heard of a student requesting a new mantra in Starling Academy history."

Cassie shrugged. It just didn't seem like such a great fit anymore. It was kind of . . . boring.

Kiri opened her mouth as if she was going to say something, clearly thought better of it, and turned to the next student. "Adora?" she said. "It's your turn."

And Adora said, "Use your logic. You are a star!"

Kiri shook her head. She was clearly getting frustrated. "Well, apparently Adora is not ready to share yet. We'll get back to you la—"

And that was when all the Star-Zaps went off. Cassie looked down at the message: SD WISH ORB IDENTIFIED. PROCEED TO LADY STELLA'S OFFICE IMMEDIATELY. The girls all shot each other quick looks, then began to make their way out of the classroom. It was time.

CHAPTER
8

Usually, when Cassie headed to Lady Stella's office for the Wish Orb reveal, her stomach was in knots. She would look at her fellow Star Darlings who had not yet been chosen for their Wish Missions and silently hope that it was their turn, instead of hers. She'd be ready, she would tell herself, next time. Just one more reprieve, and she'd be ready. But then she never was.

But this time was different. Cassie knew she was ready. And she also knew that there was no better choice for this mission than she. In fact, she was sure of it.

Cassie calmly made her way to Lady Stella's office, where she sat at the shiny silver table until all the Star Darlings were gathered. Then she patiently waited her turn as they all made their way down the hidden staircase behind Lady Stella's desk into the cool, dark secret caves underneath Halo Hall. Scarlet was just in front of her, and in the gloom Cassie noticed a silvery white bitbat land briefly on the girl's shoulder. *That's odd*, she thought. Bitbats were notoriously skittish. Soon they entered the special Star Darlings Wish Cavern. Cassie took in the scene—sunlight shining through the glass roof, golden waterfalls of wish energy streaming down the sides, the garden they stood in green and abundant. The glowing Wish Orbs still in the ground waiting for the moment when they would be ready now numbered just six. It was clearly impossible for the place to exist deep underground, yet there it was, right in front of their eyes. The girls moved to the grass-covered platform in the middle of the Wish Cavern and waited for the chosen Wish Orb to emerge. They did not have to wait long. A shaft of sunlight lit up the center of the platform and the orb burst out. Cassie never took her eyes off the glowing globe. This time, instead of circling the room quickly, or pausing at each Star Darling as if trying to decide who it belonged to, the orb simply zoomed right up to one student: Cassie. She held out one hand confidently, motioning for the orb with the other as if to say, *Get over here right now.* The Wish Orb nestled right into her open palm. Everyone stared at Cassie in disbelief.

Even Lady Stella looked very starprised. "Cassie, the Wish Orb has chosen you," she said, which seemed unnecessary, since Cassie was already cradling the glowing orb in her hands. "Are you okay?" she asked, craning her neck to look searchingly into Cassie's eyes.

"Of course," said Cassie. "Why wouldn't I be?"

As Cassie sat on her bed the morning of her mission, finalizing her arrival outfit with the help of the Wishworld Outfit Selector function on her Star-Zap, she wondered why she had feared that day so much. Everyone acted like being picked to go on a Wish Mission was such a big deal, and now that Cassie was the chosen one, it didn't seem monumental at all. For stars' sake, even Ophelia had gone on a mission. (Granted hers had been a startacularly terrible mess.) Cassie couldn't understand it. She flipped through the Wishworld outfits she had picked for the rest of her trip. They were all perfectly coordinated, down to the shoes and socks. She said her mantra to herself, annoyed that she hadn't been able to change it. "Listen to your feelings. Let your inner light sparkle," she repeated unenthusiastically. Her mantra was a dud; there was no doubt about that.

She glanced at her Star-Zap. It was time to head to the

Wishworld Surveillance Deck. She picked up her Star-Zap, then decided to send a quick holo-text to Ophelia, who she hadn't seen since that day in the Celestial Café.

Hey! I enjoyed our talk. Let's get together soon so we can start making you sparkle! I'll be in touch....

She snapped her phone shut. "Time to go?" she said to Sage, who chuckled as if Cassie had said something amusing.

"Time to go!" Sage said. "Is there any last-minute advice I can give you?"

Cassie shook her head. "No, I'm good."

★

Cassie paused for a minute in front of the glass doors that led to the Wishworld Surveillance Deck. "You go ahead," she said to Sage. She slipped a pair of safety star-glasses over her own star-shaped glasses and took stock of herself. Though she would soon be taking off into the heavens attached to a wild shooting star and landing in an unfamiliar world, she didn't feel any flutterfocuses taking flight in her belly. She looked down at her hands, which were not even close to trembling; they were as still as a piece of starmarble. She was cool, calm, and collected.

She pushed open the door and was immediately mobbed by Star Darlings wearing safety starglasses in a rainbow of colors. She looked around at everyone. Someone was missing. "Where's Libby?" she asked.

"She was still sleeping," offered Gemma. "I couldn't get her out of bed."

"Get out of here," Cassie said.

A perplexed look crossed Gemma's face. Then she shrugged. "Okay," she said. She turned around and headed inside.

Cassie started after her, but then Vega leaned in for a hug and Cassie caught a glimpse of herself in the lenses of Vega's blue safety starglasses. Cassie smiled at herself. She really did look great in white.

"So this is it," she said to Vega. "Anything to share before I go?"

"Your Wisher is now busy wishin'," Vega replied.

"That's true," said Cassie.

"Lots of luck upon your mission," Vega concluded.

"Thanks," said Cassie.

Clover stepped up and threw her arms around Cassie, nearly knocking her over. "Good luck, Cassie!" she cheered.

Adora was next. "Are you nervous, Cassie?" she said.

Huh? "Um . . . thanks," replied Cassie. She was suddenly surrounded by a group all eager to say their good-byes—Tessa, Scarlet, Leona, and then Astra. Finally, Piper stepped forward.

"Wish me luck," Cassie said to her. "Not that I—"

"Will listen!" said Piper.

"Need it," finished Cassie.

The last people to bid farewell to her were Lady Cordial and Lady Stella. Lady Cordial handed Cassie her silver backpack, and Cassie slipped it over her arm, giving the silver stuffed star a squeeze. "Star salutations," she told Lady Cordial.

Cassie stepped forward to join Lady Stella on the edge of the surveillance deck and found she couldn't move. She looked down in confusion. That's when she realized that someone had tied her shoelaces together!

"Really, Starlings?" she said as bent down to tie them properly. "That is so not funny." *Someone must be very jealous of me and my Wish Mission,* she thought. But everyone looked back at her innocently.

Lady Stella helped her to her feet and put her arm around Cassie's shoulder She pointed to the Star Wranglers throwing out their lassos made of wish energy. "You'll be on your way any starmin now," she said. She turned so she could look directly at Cassie. "And now some last-minute advice," she said, her eyes shining. "It's to trust your instincts. As I mentioned to you, your intuitive powers are startacular. And also recognize that you have the power to shape your feelings. Feeling nervous? Use your energy to turn it into excitement. But most of all, believe in yourself."

Cassie nodded. "I'm going to do a startastic job," she said.

Lady Stella nodded. "Of course you are." But Cassie thought she saw a look of starprise in her eyes. She gave Cassie a searching look that made her feel like a starquark under a holo-scope.

"You seem a little different today," Lady Stella said, a look of concern on her usually serene face.

"I am," said Cassie. "I am."

CHAPTER
9

Cassie stood in front of a large, long building, knowing that her Wisher was somewhere inside, feeling utterly miserable. It was cold, it was muddy, and it was rainy. And rain on Wishworld was nothing like the rain back home. It was decidedly unsparkly and rather than being a gentle refreshing mist it was actually quite, well, *wet*. Her clothes were soaked clean through.

With a sigh she accessed her Wishworld Outfit Selector and changed from the adorable but now sopping silver platform sandals (for height as well as fashion), light floaty white top with spaghetti straps, and pair of pink-and-white wide-legged pants that ended just below the knee into a more weather appropriate ensemble— cozy leggings; an oversized pale pink sweater, toasty as a blanket; and rubber boots. She also added a waterproof coat with a hood which she pulled up to cover her now platinum-blond hair with pale pink tips. Then she bent to fish the shooting star out of the brown muck, gave it a shake, folded it up, and placed it in her backpack, right next to her safety starglasses.

She made her first observation, which she knew would be recorded in her Cyber Journal. *Wish Mission 6, Wishworld Observation #1: Be sure to be fully prepared for all Wishworld weather conditions because you never know what you might need. You'll save yourself some time and annoyance.*

She took another deep breath and exhaled, marveling at the billowing white cloud she created. Then she squared her shoulders and marched forward in her rubbery boots. After waiting a moment for the heavy-looking metal door to slide open, she realized she had to push it to get inside. *Look out, Wisher, here I come,* she thought.

The hallway was long and appeared to be empty. Cassie stood dripping on the floor, her glasses foggy from the sudden warmth. She sighed. Wishworld was one annoyance after another so far.

"Well, hello there, young lady."

Cassie turned around quickly in the direction of the voice, and the combination of her quick movement, her slippery boots, and the wet floor caused her feet to slide right from underneath her. *Moons and stars!* she thought as her feet scrabbled on the floor, looking for purchase. The next thing she knew, she was flat on her back, staring up at the ceiling. *Oof.*

A face appeared in her line of vision—a woman's face, staring down at her and looking concerned. "Oh, my goodness, are you okay?" she asked.

"I'm fine," said Cassie with a sigh. This was not a stellar way to begin her first Wish Mission! Luckily, the only thing that was bruised was her dignity.

The woman squinted at Cassie through a small pair of glasses perched on her nose. She was clearly trying to place her—and failing. "I'm sorry," she said. "But I don't recognize you. Who are you?" She sniffed the air. "And why does it smell just like my mother's hummingbird cake?" she mused. "Boy does that take me back."

Now was as good a time as any. Cassie took off her foggy glasses and stared up into the woman's eyes. "My name is Cassie. I am the new student in school," she said. *Will it work upside down?* she wondered.

It did. "Your name is Cassie, you are the new student in school," the woman repeated as she helped Cassie to her feet. "There you go!" she said, drying her wet hands on her pant legs. "Welcome to Mountain View School, Cassie. I am Principal McIlhenney."

"Thank you," said Cassie, mentally congratulating herself for remembering the Wishling phrase for gratitude. She bent down, pretending to tuck her leggings into her boots, and stole a glance at her Star-Zap for directions to her Wisher's location. "I belong in room 261," she told the woman as she straightened up.

"You belong in room 261," the woman echoed with a nod. "That's Ms. Olds's room. I'll take you right there." She paused. "But we'll go to your new locker so you can store your things."

Cassie followed the woman down the hallway and was delighted with the small metal closet—or "locker"— she was given. There was just enough room for her dripping coat, which she was happy to dispose of. She envisioned the small top section of the locker filled with books. Paper books. *I can hardly wait to get my hands on them*, she thought.

"Ready?" asked Principal McIlhenney.

"Ready!" said Cassie, slamming her locker shut with a clang.

Cassie slung her silver backpack over her shoulder and followed the principal down the hallway. The woman paused in front of a display opposite the stairwell. Cassie looked up. There was a photo of a serious-looking girl with straight dirty-blond hair pulled back in a headband. STUDENT OF THE MONTH, it said below her photo. "Each month a student is chosen to be honored in this way," the principal said. She turned to Cassie and smiled. "Annabel here has received the award for three months running. It's awarded to a very special student who not only excels academically but also sets an example for the other students with words and actions. Maybe someday it will be you." Cassie felt a rush of warmth to her face. *Well, of course I'd be Student of the Month if I attended your school,* Cassie thought. *I'd probably be Student of the Year if that was possible!* She nodded politely and they continued up the stairs and down the hall, then stopped at the door of her new classroom. Principal McIlhenney turned to her and gave her a reassuring smile. "You'll like Ms. Olds," she said. "She's really kind and she's a good teacher."

Cassie nodded, recognizing the symbols on the classroom door from her Wishers 101 class when they had studied Wishworld holidays. They were bright green stemmed leaves with an interesting shape. "I like those . . . valentines!" she said. "Is it Halloween already?"

The principal chuckled. "Good one, Cassie!" She leaned toward her. "But Ms. Olds already has one class clown. She doesn't need another!" She rapped on the door, then turned to Cassie and smiled again. "Are you ready? Don't be nervous, now."

"Oh, I'm not nervous at all," said Cassie, giving the principal an odd glance for suggesting such a thing.

The woman looked surprised. "Good for you!" she said.

The door was opened by a kind-looking woman with medium-length brown hair. She wore a bright red sweater with white flowers on it. "Principal McIlhenney!" she said. "To what do I owe the pleasure?"

Cassie immediately filed that Wishling expression away as *Mission 6, Wishworld Observation #2. I have a great ear for charming Wishling expressions*, she thought.

The principal stepped through the doorway and a hush fell over the classroom, just like when Lady Stella made a surprise visit to a Starling Academy classroom or appeared as a multi-classroom holo-image to make an announcement. Principal McIlhenney introduced Cassie to her new teacher. While the adults talked, Cassie looked around the classroom, trying to see if she could pick out her Wisher. The students all looked back at her curiously. *Get ready, Wisher*, thought Cassie. *This is your lucky day. Your wish is about to be granted!* But although she knew the student had to be somewhere in the room, there wasn't even the tiniest flicker in her glasses—her Wish Pendant.

As Ms. Olds walked Cassie to her new desk, remarking that the air suddenly smelled like deep-dish blueberry pie, Principal McIlhenney said her good-byes and left. The class relaxed visibly after she was gone. Cassie scanned the room again. Still no glow. *That's odd*, she thought. *Could I be in the wrong classroom?* She looked at the directions on her Star-Zap. Classroom 261, just like the sign on the door. *Could my Wisher be absent?* There was one empty seat in the row next to hers in the back of the room. . . .

"Cell phones are not allowed in class," said someone in a snippy voice.

Cassie smiled at the girl, who sat in the first seat in the row next to hers. She was wearing a pale pink sweater and a plaid skirt. She was neat and tidy, not a dirty-blond hair on her head out of place.

"Thanks for the tip," said Cassie, slipping her Star-Zap into her sweater pocket. The girl stared back, unsmiling. Cassie took a closer look. "Aren't you the Student of the Month?" she said to her.

"That's me," the girl said. "Annabel Victor. And I'm going to be Student of the Month this month, too. It'll be announced at the end of the day tomorrow."

"Well, good for you," said Cassie. The girl was obnoxious, but she certainly was sure of herself; Cassie had to give her that. She sat back in her decidedly uncomfortable Wishworld seat. *I guess I'll just sit back and observe,* thought Cassie. *Blend in and get to the bottom of this Wish Mission.* She knew that she'd have it all figured out by lunchtime. She was sure of it.

She sat patiently as Ms. Olds took attendance and then asked everyone to take out their science books. Cassie was thrilled when the teacher handed her her very own copy, and she flipped through the pages excitedly. A quick glance told her that some of the information inside was hopelessly out of date, but she loved the book anyway—the weight of it in her hands, the slickness of the paper, the colorful illustrations and photographs on every page.

"Class, it's time to get out your homework," Ms. Olds said. Just as the students began to reach into their backpacks, the door burst open. There stood a tall, thin girl with long shiny black hair, clutching her books to her chest. She had a wide pleasant face and bright blue eyes that sparkled with mischief.

Cassie's glasses immediately began to glow. So this was her Wisher!

CHAPTER
18

Annabel scowled at her. "Those glasses have to be against the rules!" she said. "They're very distracting!"

"Lila, you're late," Ms. Olds scolded gently. "What happened?"

Lila looked around the room. Cassie noticed that almost all the students were staring at her with great interest, waiting to see what happened next. She shook her head dramatically, clearly enjoying the spotlight. "It was the sign!" she said. "The one down the block, at the crosswalk." She had a wide grin, and Cassie saw a flash of silver when she spoke. *Interesting*, she thought. *Could that be a clue?*

Ms. Olds shook her head, but there was a smile on

her face. "And tell us, Lila. How did a sign manage to make you late for school today?"

Lila grinned, clearly relishing the line she was about to deliver. "It said 'School Zone. Slow down.' So I did!"

The rest of the class laughed. They obviously liked Lila a lot.

"Sit down, Lila," said Ms. Olds, but in a kind way. "It's time to turn in your homework."

Lila still stood in the aisle. "Ms. Olds, would you ever get mad at me for something I didn't do?" she asked.

Ms. Olds frowned. "Of course not, Lila," she said.

"That's good, because I didn't do my homework!" said Lila. "Just kidding!"

The class burst into laughter.

"It's time to sit down, Lila," the teacher repeated.

Lila paused next to Cassie's desk on her way down the aisle. "Hey, new girl," she said. "What's your name?"

"Cassie," she replied.

"What school did you come from?" Lila asked.

That was a tough one. "Star . . . Starfield Preparatory School of . . . um . . . Preparedness," Cassie heard herself saying. *Ugh.* Why had she said that? What a ridiculous name.

But the girl laughed. "You're funny!"

Lila sat down, and the homework was collected.

Students passed their papers up the row and then the first person in each row passed them across. Ms. Olds noticed that one boy's homework was missing, though he insisted he had turned it in. But it was nowhere to be found. Finally, Ms. Olds turned on a monitor and three images were projected onto the whiteboard in the front of the room.

"Today we are going to discuss gravity. Now, who can tell me which of these photos illustrates this force?"

Several hands shot up.

"Yes, Kristie?" Ms. Olds said. "Come show us."

Kristie stood and walked to the front of the room. She pointed to a picture of a ball going through a basketball hoop. "Gravity is what pulls the ball back to the ground so it doesn't go shooting off into space," she said.

"That's right," said Ms. Olds. "Thank you, Kristie."

Kristie returned to her seat, stumbling on her way down the aisle. Cassie noticed that she gave Annabel a dirty look.

"You tripped me!" she hissed.

"Why are you looking at me?" said Annabel innocently. "I didn't do anything!"

"Settle down class," said Ms. Olds. "Now who can tell me who *discovered* gravity?"

Lila raised her hand. "I can, I can!" she said.

"Yes, Lila?" asked Ms. Olds.

"Kristie did!"

Ms. Olds sighed. "Anyone else?"

"Actually, it was . . ." Lila started.

But Annabel spoke over her. "It was Sir Isaac Newton," she said, giving Lila a disgusted look. "He published his finding in 1687," she added.

"That is correct, Annabel," said Ms. Olds. "Nicely done."

"As usual," muttered the boy who sat behind Annabel. She turned around and gave him a smirk.

Ms. Olds continued with a discussion of the force of gravity and Cassie tuned out, choosing to spend the rest of the class trying to figure out what Lila could be wishing for. She considered the evidence. She was clearly well liked by most of her classmates and she was certainly very funny. So Cassie could probably rule out a friendship wish. Could it have something to do with her family? A friend? A pet? Cassie sighed. It could be practically anything at that point.

Finally, it was time for lunch. "Annabel," said Ms. Olds. "Will you please show Cassie to the lunchroom?"

"Of course, Ms. Olds," said Annabel with a sweet smile.

Cassie followed her out of the classroom and they walked to the cafeteria in silence. Annabel paused at the entrance and turned to Cassie. Her sweet smile was gone.

"I hope you don't plan on sitting with me and my friends," she said. "Because you are definitely not invited." She turned and flounced off, waving to a group of girls already at a table.

Cassie stared after her, a look of disgust on her face. "That girl deserves a bowl of—" she looked at the menu offerings displayed on the wall behind the ladies of lunch—"vegetable chili on her head."

A voice came from beside her. "Turkey tetrazzini would be better."

Cassie spun around. It was Lila, grinning at her. "Or mac and cheese, alphabet soup, sloppy joes. But it's not worth it. You'll just get detention."

"She's so awful," said Cassie. She brightened. Maybe Lila's wish was to get even with Annabel. But how could that possibly be a good wish?

"Yeah, and the worst part is she has all the teachers fooled," said Lila. "She's been the Student of the Month three times in a row."

Cassie felt her face get warm. "That's so unfair," she said.

"Tell me about it, sister," said Lila. "Now let's get some lunch. You can sit at my table. Just keep that chili to yourself, please."

★

Cassie got in line behind Lila and took a closer look at the cafeteria. It was just as bad as Sage had said—smelly, uncomfortably warm, and filled with lots of unidentifiable food you were expected to eat.

"Do you wish to get even with Annabel?" she asked Lila.

Lila shrugged. "I wouldn't waste a wish on that. I save my wishes for important things."

Aha! thought Cassie. She grabbed a tray and a bowl of the chili. She followed Lila to a table in the back of the cafeteria, close to the windows. They had a lovely mountain view, though it wasn't quite as spectacular as the Crystal Mountains.

One by one they were joined by other girls and a couple of boys, Lila's friends. Lila introduced her to them all, and Cassie recognized several of them from room 261. They seemed like a nice bunch of kids. Cassie dug in to her chili, which was actually not inedible.

Lila told the group the story from that morning. She

was a great storyteller, and even her friends from class laughed as if they were hearing it for the first time.

"So why *were* you late this morning?" Cassie asked. Lila made a sad face and said, "It's so hard, Cassie, you wouldn't believe it if I told you. It's just so terrible. My mother . . ."

Cassie leaned forward, almost placing her chin in her pudding cup. "Yes," she breathed. She was *this close* to finding out Lila's wish; she was sure of it.

"My mother"—her voice cracked—"forgot to set the alarm last night!"

Her friends all burst into laughter. "I hate it when that happens!" a blond girl cried.

Cassie tried again. "I see your teeth are silver. Do you wish they were white?" But that got a laugh from Lila.

"You don't like my braces?" she said, baring her teeth. "Well, neither do I, but they're coming off soon."

Cassie tried again. She looked out the window at the driving rain. "Perhaps you wish for this rain to end?"

"No way," said Lila. "It's good for the plants."

She leaned back and looked at Cassie. "You ask some crazy questions, new girl," she said. "How about this one? What do you call cheese that isn't yours?"

"I have no idea," Cassie replied.

"Nacho cheese!" said Lila.

Cassie didn't get it, though the rest of the students at the table howled with laughter. "Oh," said Cassie. Another joke. She was beginning to realize that it was going to be very difficult to get Lila to be serious. How was she ever going to get the truth out of her? Just before classes began, Cassie stood up from the table and dumped her tray. She was really starting to worry and needed a moment to think, so she headed to the girls' bathroom, where she stood in front of the mirror, staring at her pale, non-sparkling reflection in the mirror. Was it time to use her underwhelming Mirror Mantra already? She pulled out her Star-Zap instead and accessed her Countdown Clock. She looked at the time remaining and gasped. It had to be broken! Could she really only have twenty-seven hours left to make Lila's wish come true? Was that even possible? Even for someone as determined and talented as she was, this was going to be tight.

★

There were no other clues for Cassie for the rest of the afternoon. And as the time came to pack up their bags, Cassie was in a bit of a panic. She couldn't let Lila out of her sight; she had to be sure to stick to her like sparkleglue for the rest of the day—and somehow wrangle an invitation to stay at her house overnight. That way she'd get extra time with her. *And I also won't have to sleep in an invisible tent in this weather*, thought Cassie. While she was pretty sure the tent was waterproof and would be warm and toasty inside, she didn't want to take any chances.

The bell rang for the end of the day and Cassie pushed into the hallway, determined not to lose sight of Lila. Luckily, the girl's locker was only a couple away from hers.

"Good first day?" Lila asked, unzipping her backpack.

"It was good," said Cassie. She decided to plunge right in. "So, um, do you want to hang out after school? Do homework together?"

"Can't," said Lila. "After-school club. Ice-dating." Or at least that was what Cassie thought she said. Her words were muffled by the arrival of a noisy bunch of kids who opened the lockers that stood between them. Cassie quickly grabbed her things, but by the time she slammed her locker shut, Lila was gone. Cassie felt her heart beat faster and her pulse race. She had to find Lila immediately.

Ice-dating? What could that be? She turned to the

girl next to her, who was staring into a mirror on the inside of the top of her locker, putting a glossy-looking substance from a tube on her lips. It smelled a bit like starberries to Cassie.

"I need to find the ice-dating club," she said.

"Ice-dating?" said the girl. "What in the world are you talking about?" Then she thought for a moment and laughed. "You mean ice-skating! Yeah, the rink is right at the bottom of the hill. Go out the front door of the school and make a left. You can't miss it."

Cassie thanked her and took off down the hall.

"It's pretty cold in there," the girl called out after her. "Don't forget your gloves!"

On the run, Cassie accessed her Wishworld Outfit Selector and made her choice. She waved her mittened hand at the girl and ran out of the school as fast as she could, whipping right past Annabel. "No running in the halls!" Annabel yelled after Cassie. "Do you hear me, new girl? Do you want a detention?"

★

Cassie pushed open the door to the ice rink. The girl had been right; it was just as cold inside as it was out. The room was huge, and a large shiny white oval stood in the middle. After some searching, Cassie found a group of students sitting on a bench, taking off their shoes. "Hey, Cassie!" said Lila with a smile. "I didn't know you were joining the ice-skating club. That's so cool!" Then she laughed at her accidental joke.

"I am!" said Cassie.

Lila introduced her to the club moderator, a teacher named Mr. Thompson. He told Cassie to take off her shoes and go get a pair of skates.

"What size?" asked the bored-looking boy behind the counter.

"One thirty-seven G," said Cassie, giving her Starland size without thinking.

The boy's eyes nearly bugged out of his head. He stared at Cassie for a minute, then grabbed her boot off the counter and turned it over. "Size five," he said, shaking his head. "Everyone's a comedian."

It took a while for Cassie to force her feet into the stiff white boots and even longer to lace them up. She stood up and quickly realized how hard it was to balance on the thin metal blades as her legs bowed first in, then out. She took a few shaky steps toward the rink, where Lila was already zipping around. A few more and she was clutching the rink wall for support. *Whew!* She made it to the entrance. The rink was a vast, intimidating expanse of white, not a sparkle in sight. Gingerly,

Cassie placed one foot on the ice, then the other. She was standing! She pushed forward confidently. While she had never skated before, she was sure that with her inherent nimbleness and ability to master new things, she'd be a natural on the ice. She glided forward and . . . *whoosh!* Within an instant she was flat on her back, looking up at the rafters. *This is the second time I've fallen since I arrived on Wishworld,* she thought. *Must be a record.*

Cassie put her hands to the ice and struggled to her feet, happy she was wearing mittens. *Moons and stars!* she thought. *This Wish Mission is more dangerous than I thought.* She somehow managed to make it to the waist-high wall that ran around the rink, and she slowly circled the rink with short, choppy steps, her hand in an iron grip on the railing. Any time she tried to let go of it, she lost her balance. She started to get hot, sweaty, and annoyed. She could see Lila zooming around the ice with her hands behind her back, then skating backward and even doing some spins. Cassie was impressed by how graceful she was.

Lila swooped toward Cassie, then turned away and sharply doubled back, sliding to a quick stop in front of her. Cassie was so startled she lost her balance. Luckily, Lila reached out a red-gloved hand and grabbed her arm in time.

"I'm sorry," Lila said. "The ice is slippery, isn't it?"

Cassie scowled at her.

"I'm not joking," she said. "It's not easy. You've got to take it slow, and pay attention. And practice."

Then, Cassie's hand firmly in hers, Lila showed her how to keep her knees bent, which dramatically improved Cassie's balance. She began to relax, a tiny bit.

"Take little steps," said Lila. "There you go. It's all about keeping your ankles steady."

Cassie wobbled forward.

"And if you think you're going to fall, make your hands into fists," she suggested. "Don't want to lose a finger under a sharp blade!"

Lila next taught Cassie how to push off and glide. And before Cassie knew it, she had navigated one full turn around the ice without falling. At the end of the hour, the girls were laughing and joking. Cassie had made it three times around the rink without falling.

She really is kind and helpful, thought Cassie. *But unfortunately I still have no idea what her wish could be.*

After the girls left the ice and had returned their skates, they put on their boots and stood outside waiting for Lila to be picked up.

"Who are you waiting for?" Cassie asked.

"My dad," said Lila.

Cassie had an idea. She hoped it would work. "Um . . . maybe you could come to my house tonight for dinner. My mom's making . . ." she searched her memory for a Wishling dinner option. "Grilled cheese pizza burgers" was what she came up with.

Lila burst out laughing. "I'd love to find out exactly what that is, but my dad is on his way to get me."

"Oh, that's too bad," said Cassie sadly. Would Lila take the bait?

She did. "Hey, why don't you come to my house for dinner instead? And sleep over, too?" she suggested. "Maybe you can have grilled cheese pizza burgers another night."

"Okay!" said Cassie quickly. Her plan had worked!

★

"What would you girls like to drink with dinner?" Lila's mother asked. She had the same black hair and easy grin as her daughter.

"Sparkling water for me," said Lila.

Cassie's eyes lit up. "Oh, yes, for me, too!" she exclaimed. Why hadn't she heard about this delightful beverage in Wishers 101? It would be a tiny reminder of home. She was missing the colors and the sparkle of Starland. It really helped to keep your spirits up, she realized. Her non-glittery surroundings were starting to get her down.

Lila's mom returned with two glasses of clear liquid, which she set on the table. A few bubbles rose to the top of each glass and popped joylessly on the surface. Cassie looked at Lila. That was it? "Um, I thought you said sparkling water," she said.

"This is sparkling water," replied Lila, taking a sip.

Cassie stared at the glass. "So where are the sparkles?" she asked.

Lila laughed. "Oh, Cassie, you crack me up!"

After dinner there were chocolate ice cream sundaes for dessert, which were startastic. But even more wonderful was that Cassie finally figured out Lila's wish.

Once the table was cleared, Cassie and Lila spread out their books on the dining room table and did their homework together. Cassie did her reading comprehension homework, reading a long passage and then answering ten multiple choice questions, and her science assignment, then dawdled over the math homework, trying to look like a normal Wishling who couldn't add, subtract, divide, and multiply huge sums instantly in her head. She stole a glance over at Lila's math book. She was pleasantly surprised to see that every answer was correct.

"Hey, you're good at math!" Cassie said admiringly.

"I am," said Lila. "Very good."

Cassie next leaned over to take a look at Lila's reading comprehension answers.

"Um," Cassie began, not sure how to broach the subject "You might want to take another look at those first . . . um . . . ten answers," she said.

Lila sucked in her cheeks and looked for a moment like she might cry. Then she glared at Cassie and slammed the book shut. "It's fine," she said tersely.

"But . . ." began Cassie.

"Just leave me alone, all right," Lila said. She stormed off and Cassie was left sitting at the dining room table by herself. She could hear Lila stomping up the stairs.

Well, this is awkward, she thought.

After giving the girl a couple of minutes to cool down, Cassie walked up the stairs, which creaked under her feet. After first opening the doors to two closets and a bathroom, she spotted a door with a sign on it that said LILA'S ROOM.

She grinned. "I'm a regular Detective Marmaduke Carbuncle," she said to herself. She took a deep breath and knocked on Lila's door.

"Come in," said a muffled voice.

Cassie opened the door. Lila was lying on her bed, her face buried in a pillow.

Cassie sat gingerly on the edge of the bed. "Do you want to talk?" she said.

With a heavy sigh, Lila flipped over on her back and stared at the ceiling, unable to make eye contact with Cassie.

"So now you know," she said. "I'm great at math but I'm terrible at reading," she said. "It's so humiliating. Ms. Olds must think I'm so dumb."

Cassie felt a sudden tingly rush of energy. She shivered with excitement. "You wish Ms. Olds would appreciate you," she said, her eyes shining.

Lila sat up, clutching the pillow to her chest. "I want her to like me," she said. "So to get her attention, I try to make her laugh. But she ends up getting mad at me." She sighed. "Meanwhile, people like Annabel Victor get all the attention. It's not fair."

"Well, I have a suggestion," said Cassie. "Save the jokes for lunch and recess. Just be your smart, kind, helpful self during the school day. Like when you helped me today at the ice rink. Ms. Olds is sure to notice and appreciate you."

Lila got a hopeful look on her face. "You really think so?"

"I do," replied Cassie. "And here's another thing. I'm pretty good at reading. I can give you some tips to help with this reading comprehension stuff. You might never be as good at it as math, but you could get better," she told her. "It's kind of like ice skating. Take it slow. Pay attention. Practice, practice, practice. Use a dictionary when you get to words you don't know." She laughed. "Okay, that's not like ice skating, but you catch my gift."

"I catch your *drift*," corrected Lila.

"See, you're paying attention already," said Cassie. Though she thought her way made more sense.

The two girls got ready for bed.

Before Lila drifted off to sleep she asked, "Do you really think this plan to impress Ms. Olds is going to work?"

"I'm sure of it," Cassie said confidently. *With me on the case*, she thought, *how could it* not *work?*

CHAPTER
11

They had pancakes for breakfast the next morning. They looked just like starcakes to Cassie, only round. They tasted pretty similar, too. Cassie tried maple syrup for the first time and nearly poured the whole container onto her plate, it was so delicious. *Tessa would love this on her starberry waffles,* she thought.

"Do you remember the plan?" she asked Lila. "Plenty of participation, kindness, and generosity. Today and every day. There are much more positive ways of getting attention from your teacher."

Lila bit her lip. "I'm a little nervous!"

"No need to be nervous," said Cassie. "Just be yourself." Then she hastily added, "Maybe without quite as many jokes, of course!"

Lila held her glass of orange juice up to Cassie. "To participation, kindness, generosity, and no jokes," she said. Cassie stared at her blankly. "Pick up your glass," instructed Lila. "Let's make a toast!" Cassie held her juice aloft and Lila clinked hers against it. And Cassie made another Wishworld observation: *"Toast" has more than one meaning on Wishworld!*

There was just one problem with the plan—Annabel. Cassie knew that they only had six hours left to make Lila's wish come true and the girl thwarted them at every turn. When Lila patiently raised her hand to answer a difficult math problem, Annabel shouted out the answer. When Ms. Olds walked into the classroom with a big stack of books in her arms, and Lila raced to the front of the room to help her, Annabel leaned over and give Lila a little push so she accidentally knocked the books to the floor. Annabel then made a big show out of helping the teacher pick them up. And Cassie stewed when Ms. Olds gave Annabel a grateful smile.

"Class, please pass your homework forward," Ms. Olds said. Everyone reached into their folders and handed their work to the person in front of them. Ms.

Olds collected the sheets from the first person in each row and stacked them together. She flipped through the pages at her desk. "Lila, I don't see yours, did you forget to hand it in?" she asked.

Lila looked up, confused. "No," she said. "I handed it in."

Ms. Olds looked again. "I don't see it here," she said.

Lila looked at Cassie nervously. Then instinct must have kicked in. To Cassie's dismay she started to say, "Hey, Ms. Olds, would you get mad if . . ."

Cassie knew what was coming next. She shook her head at Lila. *No jokes!* she thought. Not realizing exactly what she was doing, she willed Lila's voice to lower in volume. And that's exactly what happened. Lila's mouth was moving, but no sound was coming out.

Wow, thought Cassie. I guess I found my secret talent. She practiced on the next student who raised her hand.

"Ms. Olds, may I please be excused?" the girl said, her voice increasing in volume with each word. She looked surprised.

Cassie stared daggers at Annabel, who was sitting primly at her desk, her hands clasped together. She knew the girl had to be the one who took Lila's homework. She pretended to be one thing, but was actually quite just the opposite. And she had all the grown-ups fooled.

★

The bell rang for lunch. Lila shook her head as she walked out of the classroom with Cassie. "Well, that didn't go so well," she said. "And what do you think happened to my homework?"

But then Lila caught a look at Cassie's disappointed face. "Come on," she said, trying to cheer Cassie up. "No need to look so upset. It's no big deal."

Cassie's Countdown Clock told her differently. She was running out of time. It really *was* a big deal. Cassie waved Lila off. "I'll see you in the cafeteria," she said. She looked around grumpily. Where was Ms. Olds now to see how sweet and understanding Lila was? But the hallway was empty. She looked again. Oh, no, it wasn't. There, across the hall, staring back at her, was Scarlet. She was still sparkly (at least to Cassie) but she was wearing leggings and a large black sweater that looked like it had been eaten by moonmoths over a bright pink shirt that peeked through all the holes. Her hair was almost entirely black (with pink bangs). But it was Scarlet just the same. And Cassie knew exactly what that meant.

"I know, I know," said Cassie, shaking her head. "My wish is in serious trouble."

"So what's going on?" asked Scarlet. "Lady Stella is really worried. You know you're running out of time on the Countdown Clock, right?"

Cassie told Scarlet the whole story.

"Oh, that Annabel sounds awful," said Scarlet. "So what are we going to do?"

"We have to figure out a way to help Lila look good in front of Ms. Olds," said Cassie. "Before the end of the school day, which is when the Countdown Clock will run out."

"Well, you'd better figure it out fast," said Scarlet.

Cassie thought for a moment. "Can you go down to the principal's office and tell her you're the new girl in class 261?"

Scarlet nodded. "And then what?"

Cassie shrugged. "And then she'll bring you upstairs and then . . ." her voice trailed off. "And then we'll figure something out."

"Okay," said Scarlet. She skipped down the hallway, then stopped and looked back. "I hope you know what you are doing," she said.

Cassie smiled and waved. She'd figure it out. She was sure of it.

★

"You never came to lunch," said Lila, when she found Cassie standing in the hallway outside of the classroom. "You must be hungry. I brought you a snack." She handed Cassie a bag of some odd-looking twisty brown things. "Thank you," said Cassie eagerly, tearing open the bag. She was hungry. "So can you continue to not tell jokes in class?" she asked.

Lila stared at the floor. "It's hard," she said.

"Tell me a joke," said Cassie. "Get it out of your system!"

Lila looked up. "Why was the math book sad?" she asked.

"I don't know," said Cassie "Why?"

Lila grinned. "Because it had so many problems," she said.

The two girls laughed. Then Lila grew serious. "Cassie, I don't know if this is going to work. I don't think Ms. Olds is ever going to take me seriously as a student."

"Hey, would you humor me for a minute?' asked Cassie.

Lila nodded.

Cassie grabbed her hand. "Sometimes when I need

strength and reassurance, I say these words out loud. It just makes me feel better and gives me focus." And then, even though she was not particularly fond of her mantra, she said it out loud: "Listen to your feelings. Let your inner light sparkle." A tingle ran through Cassie. Lila must have felt it, too, because her eyes widened. "Wow," she said. "I *do* feel better."

Annabel came bustling over to them. "No eating in the hallway," she said. She grabbed the pretzels from Cassie's hand and tossed them into the trash.

"I was hungry," said Cassie. "And that was mean. I'm . . . I'm going to tell Ms. Olds."

"Like she's really going to believe you over me, three-time Student of the Month?" Annabel scoffed. She turned to Lila and gave her a cruel smile. "What ever happened to your homework?" she asked.

"I bet I can guess," said Lila.

"You'll never prove it," answered Annabel.

With a sigh, Cassie and Lila headed into the classroom. Cassie had no idea what she was going to do when Scarlet arrived. But still, she was certain it was going to be good.

CHAPTER
12

Scarlet stood in front of the class, doing her best to look like a new Wishling student. She looked at her feet and smiled shyly when the principal introduced her to Ms. Olds, who remarked (again) that she smelled deep-dish blueberry pie. Scarlet gave Cassie a look which plainly said "So, what do we do now?" Cassie was still not sure, so she shrugged. They'd have to play it by year, a new Wishling expression she had picked up on her mission. She assumed that meant they would make it up as they went along.

"Ms. Olds," said Principal McIlhenney, "will you join me outside for a moment?"

"Certainly," said Ms. Olds. "Scarlet, please take the

seat next to Annabel for today." She smiled. "Annabel, I'm sure you'll do your best to make our newest student feel welcome."

As soon as the adults stepped into the hallway, Scarlet skipped across the room to her seat. Cassie watched as Annabel's eyes lit up. Annabel turned to Scarlet, a mocking look on her face. Suddenly, Cassie knew exactly what to do. She concentrated, dialing up the volume. She just hoped it would be loud enough for the adults to hear.

"Did you just skip?" Annabel said mockingly. "What, are we in preschool?" Her amplified voice echoed in the classroom, but her eyes were flashing and she didn't seem to notice.

Scarlet stopped in her tracks. "Are you talking to me?" she said.

"Yes, I'm talking to you," Annabel replied. "Skipping like a baby."

Scarlet honestly looked confused. "I have no idea what you're talking about. I would never *skip*," she said hotly. "I was hurrying."

Annabel laughed. "Oh, yes you were. And those clothes. Did you get that sweater at a garage sale or something? I mean, really."

Scarlet was staring daggers at Annabel, looking like

she was about to start yelling at her. Then someone spoke up. It was Lila.

"Enough," she said, standing and walking up the aisle. "Leave the poor girl alone."

"Poor girl?" said Scarlet, clearly puzzled.

"Ms. Olds asked you to welcome Scarlet into our classroom," she said, two spots of pink in her cheeks. Noticing her voice was extra loud, she tried to lower it. But Cassie turned up the volume as loud as she could. "We are supposed to treat our classmates with respect. Be kind to them. And you did neither. You were just plain mean." She turned to Scarlet. "Welcome to our class, Scarlet. We're not all like Annabel," she said. "Actually, we're all pretty nice. I think you're going to like it here."

Just then there was the sound of clapping. Cassie spun around to look at the doorway. And there she saw Ms. Olds and Principal McIlhenney, applauding Lila.

"Nicely done, Lila," said Ms. Olds. "You are a wonderful example of a good citizen and supportive classmate." She turned to Annabel and shook her head. "And Annabel, I am shocked, simply shocked, by your behavior toward our newest student. It is simply unacceptable."

Annabel stared down at her desk in a furious silence. Cassie got the idea that her mean girl days were over.

The principal was beaming. "Lila, your behavior was a great example for the rest of the students. Exactly the way our new Student of the Month should act."

Lila nodded and smiled. "Lila," said Cassie. "Principal McIlhenney just said that you're the Student of the Month!"

"What?" said Lila with a gasp. "Are you serious? Me?"

The principal nodded. "Congratulations!"

The class, everyone except for Annabel that is, cheered.

"Student of the Month," Lila said to herself. "I can't believe it." Everyone could see the joy on her face, but only Cassie and Scarlet could see the glimmering rainbow waves of pure wish energy that arced through the air. Cassie almost ducked when they flew right at her face, but then she stood still as they were absorbed by her star-shaped glasses. She closed her eyes and felt the warmth and positive feelings flow through her.

When the bell rang for the end of the day, Lila rushed up to Cassie and hugged her so tightly she lifted her off the ground. "Thank you, Cassie!" she said, her eyes shining. Cassie hugged her back, which she knew would erase Lila's—and everyone's—memory of her visit.

When they broke apart, Lila had a strange, distant look on her face. She blinked and then walked out of the classroom, not turning back. They hadn't even had a chance to say good-bye. And Cassie, with a large lump in her throat, thought it was better that way.

Epilogue

"Star salutations," said Cassie as she walked into Lady Stella's office and was immediately surrounded by her fellow Star Darlings, all eager to congratulate her. "It wasn't easy, but I ended up doing a startacular job, if I do say so myself," she said.

Scarlet cleared her throat. "And?"

Cassie clapped Scarlet on the back, hoping she looked modest and generous as she did so. "Oh, yes, and of course Scarlet was really just so helpful to me. Star salutations, Scarlet."

Scarlet nodded. "You're welcome," she said. Then she smiled. "That was a pretty crazy mission. Why that girl accused me of skipping, I'll never know."

Everyone took their seats around Lady Stella's silver

table, but Cassie stayed standing, knowing what was about to happen. Lady Stella handed the Wish Orb to Cassie. Cassie felt a lump in her throat as she stared at the beautiful glowing ball of light. Then she gasped as it began to transform into a silverbella, its round blossom a cluster of tiny stars shining with moonglow. She stared at it for a moment, transfixed. Then the stars parted to reveal a stunning cluster of pale pink jewels—a lunalite, Cassie's Power Crystal.

"Oh," she breathed. "It's the most beautiful Power Crystal of them all."

"It is lovely," said Lady Stella. "But they're all beautiful, Cassie."

Cassie looked up and gave the headmistress a wink. *As if!* She turned to her fellow Star Darlings, who, she felt, all seemed to be waiting for her to say a few words. "My fellow Star Darlings," she began. "Although my mission was most probably the best one of all so far— no offense to the rest of you—I want to tell you that success did not come as easily to me as you may imagine. I think I can be a shining example to you all as I persevered—"

"Star salutations, Cassie," interrupted Lady Stella. "But I think we're done here." She was staring at her, Cassie imagined, with great admiration. After all, Cassie had taken the headmistress's words to heart. She had turned her fear into total confidence. And just in time for her mission, too.

★

Cassie stayed behind to chat a bit with Lady Stella, who kept asking her if she was okay. She was fine, she said. She was startastic. What was the problem?

When she got back to her room, she placed her hand on the palm scanner. "Welcome back, Cassie," said the Bot-Bot voice. "And good job!"

"Star salutations," she said distractedly.

Her room was filled with Star Darlings. Astra was bouncing her star ball against the wall. Tessa was braiding Gemma's hair. Adora was browsing through Cassie's huge collection of holo-books. Libby was sleeping on her window seat.

"Star greetings, everyone," said Cassie. "And star salutations for coming here today. I have some important things to discuss with you, my fellow Star Darlings. As you know, I am a very sensitive and thoughtful individual. I often see things that many of you might miss. As a matter of fact . . ."

"Get to the point!" someone called out.

"Fine," said Cassie. "I called you all here because

something weird is going on at Starling Academy. And it involves us, the Star Darlings. I told Vega I would wait until I had proof, and now I think I do."

"What is it?" asked Leona. "Does it have to do with my messed-up mission?"

"And Scarlet being kicked out of the Star Darlings?" asked Astra.

"Yes," said Cassie. "There are a lot of weird things going on around campus, and I think the clues all lead to one individual."

"Who?" said Leona.

"Yes, tell us!" Astra shouted.

"Ophelia," said Cassie.

"I knew it!" Scarlet shouted.

"Something just isn't right," said Cassie. "She talks about her mom in the present tense. She's an orphan but she gets care packages. How could she have been admitted to Starling Academy if she was so clueless? Something is off with her. I don't think she's an orphan and I don't think she's clueless at all. I didn't put it all together until my Wish Mission. I met a girl who was pretending to be something she wasn't. I think Ophelia is doing the same thing."

"Well, I don't believe it," said Leona stubbornly. "I

think you are being unfair. I'm going to her room right now to straighten this out once and for all."

"I'm coming with you," said Scarlet, scrambling to her feet.

But Leona continued to sit on the bed. After a few moments, Scarlet grabbed her hand and dragged her out the door. The rest of the Star Darlings (save the still napping Libby) were close behind.

They hopped on the Cosmic Transporter, everyone tensely silent, and made their way to Ophelia's new room. Leona knocked and knocked on the door. There was no answer.

"Ophelia!" she called. "It's Leona." She turned to Cassie, her face flushed golden. "I asked you to look out for her, not investigate her!"

There was no answer. Finally, Scarlet skipped off to get a Bot-Bot guard. When they told it that they were worried about Ophelia, it finally relented and opened the door for them.

Leona barged into the room first and let out a gasp.

"What's wrong?" Cassie shouted, pushing her way inside. She looked around, bewildered. Ophelia was gone. The room was empty. There was not a thing in it. It was as if no one had ever lived there.

But on the wall, in hastily scribbled yellow letters, were the words *I'M SORRY.*

"This is terrible," Gemma said.

"You can say that again," said Cassie.

"This is terrible," Gemma repeated.

And then nobody said anything else, because they were plunged into a sudden and total darkness. For the first time in Starland history, the lights had gone out.

Glossary

Aeropuff: A Starland dessert.

Afterglow: The Starling afterlife. When Starlings die, it is said that they have "begun their afterglow."

Age of Fulfillment: The age when a Starling is considered mature enough to begin to study wish granting.

Bad Wish Orbs: Orbs that are the result of bad or selfish wishes made on Wishworld. These grow dark and warped and are quickly sent to the Negative Energy Facility.

Ballum blossom tree: A Starland tree with cherry blossom–like flowers that light up at night.

Big Dipper Dormitory: Where third- and fourth-year students live.

Boingtree gum: Starland chewing gum.

Bot-Bot: A Starland robot. There are Bot-Bot guards, waiters, deliverers, and guides on Starland.

Bright Day: The date a Starling is born, celebrated each year like a Wishling birthday.

Celestial Café: Starling Academy's outstanding cafeteria.

Cloudcandy: Name for various Starland confections.

Cocomoon: A sweet and creamy fruit with an iridescent glow.

Comet Prep: A rival of Starling Academy in star ball.

Cosmic Transporter: The moving sidewalk system that transports students through dorms and across the Starling Academy campus.

Countdown Clock: A timing device on a Starling's Star-Zap. It lets them know how much time is left on a Wish Mission, which coincides with when the Wish Orb will fade.

Crystal Mountains: The most beautiful mountains on Starland. They are located across the lake from Starling Academy.

Cycle of Life: A Starling's life span. When Starlings die, they are said to have "completed their Cycle of Life."

Drifting moonbug: A storytelling device meant to mislead the reader. Starland's version of a red herring.

Druderwomp: An edible barrel-like bush capable of pulling up its own roots and rolling like a tumbleweed, then planting itself again.

Featherwhisper: A Starland dessert.

Floating Wisp: A Starland dessert.

Flutterfocus: A Starland creature similar to a Wishworld butterfly but with illuminated wings.

Galliope: A sparkly Starland creature similar to a Wishworld horse.

Garble greens: A Starland vegetable similar to spinach.

Glitterberries: A sweet Starland fruit.

Globerbeem: Large, friendly lightning bug–type insects that are sparkly and lay eggs.

Glorange: A glowing orange fruit. Its juice is often enjoyed at breakfast time.

Glowfur: A small, furry Starland creature with gossamer wings that eats flowers and glows.

Good Wish Orbs: Orbs that are the result of positive wishes made on Wishworld. They are planted in Wish-Houses.

Gossamerwisp: A Starland dessert.

Green Globules: Green pellets that are fed to pet glowfurs. They don't taste very good to Starlings.

Half-moon pie: A Starland dessert.

Halo Hall: The building where Starling Academy classes are held.

Holo-dice: A holographic version of dice.

Holo-text: A message received on a Star-Zap and projected into the air. There are also holo-albums, holo-billboards, holo-books, holo-cards, holo-communications, holo-diaries, holo-flyers, holo-letters, holo-papers, holo-pictures, and holo–place cards. Anything that would be made of paper or contain writing or images on Wishworld is a hologram on Starland.

Hydrong: The equivalent of a Wishworld hundred.

Illuminated Manuscript Technology: Also known as IMT, a new technology allowing a reader to view the action in a holo-book as the book is read aloud.

Impossible Wish Orbs: Orbs that are the result of wishes made on Wishworld that are beyond the power of Starlings to grant.

Isle of Misera: A barren rocky island off the coast of New Prism.

Lightning Lounge: A place on the Starling Academy campus where students relax and socialize.

Little Dipper Dormitory: Where first- and second-year students live.

Luminous Lake: A serene and lovely lake next to the Starling Academy campus.

Luminous Library: The impressive library at Starling Academy.

Meepletile: A Starland creature closest in nature to a Wishworld reptile. It frequently sheds its skin.

Mirror Mantra: A saying specific to each Star Darling that when recited gives her (and her Wisher) reassurance and strength. When a Starling recites her Mirror Mantra while looking in a mirror, she will see her true appearance reflected.

Moonium: An amount similar to a Wishworld million.

Old Prism: A medium-sized historical city about an hour from Starling Academy.

Power Crystal: The powerful stone that each Star Darling receives once she has granted her first wish.

Purple piphany: A Starland flower with a distinctive fragrance.

Shooting stars: Speeding stars that Starlings can latch on to and ride to Wishworld.

Silverbella: An orb-shaped Starland flower with tiny pink and white petals that radiate from its center.

Silver Blossom: The final manifestation of a Good Wish Orb. This glimmering metallic bloom is placed in the Hall of Granted Wishes.

Solar Springs: A hilly small town in the countryside where Tessa and Gemma are from.

Sparkle shower: An energy shower Starlings take every day to get clean and refresh their sparkling glow.

Star ball: An intramural sport that shares similarities with soccer on Wishworld. But star ball players use energy manipulation to control the ball.

Starbounce: Starland's version of a trampoline.

Starcar: The primary mode of transportation for most Starlings. These ultrasafe vehicles drive themselves on cushions of wish energy.

Star Caves: The caverns underneath Starling Academy where the Star Darlings' secret Wish-Cavern is located.

Starf!: A Starling expression of dismay.

Star flash: News bulletin, often used starcastically.

Starland City: The largest city on Starland, also its capital.

Starlicious: Tasty, delicious.

Starlings: The glowing beings with sparkly skin who live on Starland.

Starmarble: An attractive stone used for surfaces in Starland architecture.

Starpillows: A Starland dessert.

Star Quad: The center of the Starling Academy campus. The dancing fountain, band shell, and hedge maze are located here.

Star salutations: The Starling way to say "thank you."

Staryear: A period of 365 days on Starland, the equivalent of a Wishworld year.

Star-Zap: The ultimate smartphone that Starlings use for all communications. It has myriad features.

Stellar School: A rival of Starling Academy in star ball.

Stellation: The point of a star. Halo Hall has five stellations, each housing a different department.

Supernova: A stellar explosion. Also used colloquially, meaning "really angry," as in "She went supernova when she found out the bad news."

Time of Letting Go: One of the four seasons on Starland. It falls between the warmest season and the coldest, similar to fall on Wishworld.

Time of Lumiere: The warmest season on Starland, similar to summer on Wishworld.

Time of New Beginnings: Similar to spring on Wishworld, this is the season that follows the coldest time of year; it's when plants and trees come into bloom.

Time of Shadows: The coldest season of the year on Starland, similar to winter on Wishworld.

Toothlight: A high-tech gadget that Starlings use to clean their teeth.

Wish Blossom: The bloom that appears from a Wish Orb after its wish is granted.

Wish energy: The positive energy that is released when a wish is granted. Wish energy powers everything on Starland.

Wisher: The Wishling who has made the wish that is being granted.

Wish-Granters: Starlings whose job is to travel down to Wishworld to help make wishes come true and collect wish energy.

Wish-House: The place where Wish Orbs are planted and cared for until they sparkle. Once the orb's wish is granted, it becomes a Wish Blossom.

Wishlings: The inhabitants of Wishworld.

Wish Mission: The task a Starling undertakes when she travels to Wishworld to help grant a wish.

Wish Orb: The form a wish takes on Wishworld before traveling to Starland. There it will grow and sparkle when it's time to grant the wish.

Wish Pendant: A gadget that absorbs and transports wish energy, helps Starlings locate their Wishers, and changes a Starling's appearance. Each Wish Pendant holds a different special power for its Star Darling.

Wishworld: The planet Starland relies on for wish energy. The beings on Wishworld know it by another name—Earth.

Wishworld Outfit Selector: A program on each Star-Zap that accesses Wishworld fashions for Starlings to wear to blend in on their Wish Missions.

Wishworld Surveillance Deck: Located high above the campus, it is where Starling Academy students go to observe Wishlings through high-powered telescopes.

Zing: A traditional Starling breakfast drink. It can be enjoyed hot or iced.

Acknowledgments

It is impossible to list all of our gratitude, but we will try.

Our most precious gift and greatest teacher, Halo; we love you more than there are stars in the sky . . . punashaku. To the rest of our crazy, awesome, unique tribe—thank you for teaching us to go for our dreams. Integrity. Strength. Love. Foundation. Family. Grateful. Mimi Muldoon—from your star doodling to naming our Star Darlings, your artistry, unconditional love, and inspiration is infinite. Didi Muldoon—your belief and support in us is only matched by your fierce protection and massive-hearted guidance. Gail. Queen G. Your business sense and witchy wisdom are legendary. Frank—you are missed and we know you are watching over us all. Along with Tutu, Nana, and Deda, who are always present, gently guiding us in spirit. To our colorful, totally genius, and bananas siblings—Patrick, Moon, Diva, and Dweezil—there is more creativity and humor in those four names than most people experience in a lifetime. Blessed. To our magical nieces—Mathilda, Zola, Ceylon, and Mia—the Star Darlings adore you and so do we. Our witchy cuzzie fairy godmothers—Ane and Gina. Our fairy fashion godfather, Paris. Our sweet Panay. Teeta and Freddy—we love you all so much. And our four-legged fur babies—Sandwich, Luna, Figgy, and Pinky Star.

The incredible Barry Waldo, our SD partner. Sent to us from above in perfect timing. Your expertise and friendship are beyond words. We love you and Gary to the moon and back. Long live the manifestation room!

Catherine Daly—the stars shined brightly upon us the day we aligned with you. Your talent and inspiration are otherworldly; our appreciation cannot be expressed in words. Many heartfelt hugs for you and the adorable Oonagh.

To our beloved Disney family. Thank you for believing in us. Wendy Lefkon, our master guide and friend through this entire journey. Stephanie Lurie, for being the first to believe in Star Darlings. Suzanne Murphy, who helped every step of the way. Jeanne Mosure, we fell in love with you the first time we met, and Star Darlings wouldn't be what it is without you. Andrew Sugerman, thank you so much for all your support.

Our team . . . Devon (pony pants) and our Monsterfoot crew—so grateful. Richard Scheltinga—our angel and protector. Chris Abramson—thank you! Special appreciation to Richard Thompson, John LaViolette, Swanna, Mario, and Sam.

To our friends old and new—we are so grateful to be on this rad journey that is life with you all. Fay. Jorja. Chandra. Sananda. Sandy. Kathryn. Louise. What wisdom and strength you share. Ruth, Mike, and the rest of our magical Wagon Wheel bunch—how lucky we are. How inspiring you are. We love you.

Last—we have immeasurable gratitude for every person we've met along our journey, for all the good and the bad; it is all a gift. From the bottom of our hearts we thank you for touching our lives.

Shana Muldoon Zappa is a jewelry designer and writer who was born and raised in Los Angeles. She has an endless imagination and a passion to inspire positivity through her many artistic endeavors. She and her husband, Ahmet Zappa, collaborated on Star Darlings especially for their magical little girl and biggest inspiration, Halo Violetta Zappa.

Ahmet Zappa is the *New York Times* best-selling author of *Because I'm Your Dad* and *The Monstrous Memoirs of a Mighty McFearless.* He writes and produces films and television shows and loves pancakes, unicorns, and making funny faces for Halo and Shana.

Sneak Peek

Piper's Perfect Dream

In her Little Dipper Dorm room, Piper finished her last holo-text. Then she swiped the screen on her Star-Zap to queue up all the messages. Star Kindness Day was the next day. A ceremony would be held in the morning, at precisely the moment the nighttime stars and the daytime sun could all be seen in the color-streaked sky.

It happened in the morning only once a staryear. And all over Starland, Starlings met in open areas to gaze at the sight. Light energy flowed. Everyone smiled. They exchanged positive messages then and for the rest of the day—to loved ones, to strangers, and to everyone in between. Thoughtful compliments. Meaningful praise. Heartfelt affirmations. It was definitely Piper's favorite holiday.

At Starling Academy, all the students' messages would go out at once, while everyone gathered in the Star Quad before class. Piper checked her holo-texts one last time. She had her own holiday tradition: styling her compliments into poetry. What better way to get a loving message across, she felt, than using language that lifted the spirit, too?

That staryear, she'd worked especially hard on the poems. There had been many ups and downs for the Star Darlings. So much had happened already that year. All the SD missions—some successful, some not. So that day, of all days, Piper wanted her friends to feel good.

Finally pleased with her efforts, Piper tossed her Star-Zap onto a neat pile of pillows on the floor. She'd played around with poetry ideas for starweeks. *Should I use lightkus?* she'd wondered first.

That poetry originated from Lightku Isle, an isolated island with sandy, sparkling beaches, where the local Starlings spoke solely in those kinds of poems, spare and simple with only three lines of verse and seventeen syllables total.

How they managed this without even trying was a wonder to Piper. She herself strove for an effortless state of being on a stardaily basis. But the lightkus proved too difficult and limiting. So Piper went with sunnets, rhyming poems that could be any length and meter but needed to include a source of light.

The last staryear, when Piper was a relatively new first-year student, the holiday hadn't gone quite the way she'd wanted. She had labored long and hard over those holo-texts then, too. She'd wanted to reach out to every single student at Starling Academy. She'd wanted each student to feel good after reading her text; appreciated, even loved, she'd hoped.

She wrote one epic poem but it turned out to be so long and so serious no one bothered reading it. A hot flash of energy coursed through Piper, just remembering it. She'd felt like crying for stardays after.

This staryear, she was determined to get it right. She decided to focus only on students she knew well, and that meant mostly the Star Darlings. She tried to make the poems fun and light, too. Zippy, you might say. No one would think Piper particularly zippy, she knew. She tended to move slowly and unhurriedly, taking in her surroundings to be fully in the moment. But of course she had her own inner energy. And maybe this year she managed to get that across in her poetry.

Piper leaned back against her soft pillow, closed her

eyes, and visualized each of her friends' smiling faces as they read her special words of encouragement. Well, maybe Scarlet and Leona wouldn't exactly be smiling. Even with her failed mission well in the past and band rehearsals on again, Leona was just beginning to bounce back.

As for Scarlet, she'd had an amazing kind of mission. After being booted out of the Star Darlings, she'd brought back wish energy and basically saved her substitute SD, Ophelia, in the bargain.

Still, it was hard to get a read on Scarlet. Piper wasn't sure what the older Starling was really thinking. One thing was crystal clear, though: Scarlet didn't like rooming with Leona. And Leona felt the same about Scarlet. Even when those poisonous flowers were removed from the girls' dorm rooms so they couldn't spread negativity, those two just couldn't get along.

Yes, there was a lot happening at the academy, and on Starland itself. That recent blackout after Cassie's mission, for instance, had thrown everyone off balance. Even the teachers weren't immune. Headmistress Lady Stella, usually so calm and serene—and an inspiration to Piper—seemed a little edgy. And the head of admissions, Lady Cordial, was stammering and hemming and hawing more than usual.

Now, more than ever, everyone needed to be centered and positive. So really, this was the perfect time for Star Kindness Day.

As Piper thought about everything, her stomach did an unexpected flip. Maybe she should send a positive poem to herself! She stretched to pick up her Star-Zap without lifting her head, then tapped the self-holo-text feature.

Piper's picture popped up in the corner of the screen: a serene, faraway expression on her face, thin seafoam-green eyebrows matching long straight seafoam-green hair, and big green eyes looking into the distance.

For the holo-photo, Piper had pulled her hair back in a ponytail. The ends reached well below her waist. Her expression was as calm as when she swam in Luminous Lake. And that was how she wanted to feel now. Centered and peaceful and wonderfully relaxed. What poem would bring her that mind-set?

Like the calm at the center of the storm . . . Piper began writing. Then she paused. What rhymed with *storm*? *The Little Dipper Dorm*, where first and second years lived!

> *Like the calm at the center of the storm,*
> *Floating like a breeze through the Little Dipper Dorm.*

Again, Piper stopped to think.

With dreams as your guiding light . . .

(Piper was a big believer in dreams holding life truths.)

Your thoughts bring deep insight.

It wasn't her best work, Piper knew. But it was getting late and she was growing tired. Piper liked to get the most sleep possible. After all, it was the startime of day when the body and mind regrouped and reconnected. Sure, she'd had her regular afternoon nap, but sometimes that just wasn't enough.

Piper focused on dimming the lights, and a starsec later, the white light faded to a soft, comforting shade of green, conducive to optimal rest. Piper shared a room with Vega, but each girl's side was uniquely her own.

Piper knew Vega was getting ready for bed, too. But it felt like she had her own secluded space, far removed from her roommate and the hustle and bustle of school. Everything was soft and fluid here. There wasn't one sharp edge in sight.

Piper's water bed was round; her pillows (dozens of them) were round. Her feathery ocean-blue throw rug and matching comforter were round. Even her leafy green plants were in pretty round bowls. And each one gave off a soothing scent that calmed and renewed her.

"Sleep tight, good night, don't let the moonbugs bite," Vega called out.

"Starry dreams," Piper replied softly. She heard Vega opening and closing drawers, neatening everything into well-organized groups, and stacking holo-books in her orderly way. Everyone had their own sleep rituals, Piper knew, and she did admire the way Vega kept her side neat. A place for everything, and everything in its place.

Piper reached to the floor, scooping up another pillow—this one had turquoise tassels and a pattern of swirls—and tucking it behind her head. Then she realized with a start she was still wearing her day clothes: a long sleeveless dress made from glimmerworm silk. It could, in fact, pass as a nightgown. Piper's day clothes weren't all that different from her night ones. But Piper believed in the mind-body connection—in this case, changing clothes to change her frame of mind.

Piper slipped on a satiny nightgown, with buttons as soft as glowmoss running from top to bottom. Then she misted the room with essence of dramboozle, a natural herb that promoted sweet dreams and comforting sleep. Next in her bedtime ritual came the choosing of the sleep mask. That night she sifted through her basket of masks, choosing one that pictured a stand of gloak trees.

It was a wonderful balance of strength and beauty, Piper thought.

Finally, Piper picked up her latest dream diary. She wanted to replay her last dream—the one from her afternoon nap. Frequently, those dreams were her most vivid. At night Piper listened to class lectures while she slept, studying in the efficient Starling method. And sometimes the professors' voices blended with her dreams in an oddly disconcerting way.

Once, she felt on the verge of a mighty epiphany—a revelation about the meaning of light. *What is the meaning of light?* was a question that had plagued Starling scholars for hydrongs and hydrongs of years. And the answer was about to be revealed. To her!

But just when Piper's thoughts were closing in on it, her Astral Accounting teacher's voice interrupted, monotonously intoning the number 1,792. And Piper felt sure that wasn't the right answer.

But that afternoon's dream proceeded without numbers or facts or formulas: Piper was floating through space, traveling past planets and stars, when a Wishling girl with bright shiny eyes and an eager expression grabbed her hand. Suddenly, the scene shifted to the Crystal Mountains, the most beautiful in all of Starland, just across the lake from Starling Academy. It was a sight

Piper looked at with pleasure every starday. But now she was climbing a mountain, still holding hands with the girl. As she led the way up a trail, the lulling sound of keytar music echoed everywhere, and she laughed with pleasure as a flutterfocus landed on her shoulder. Another flutterfocus settled on the shoulder of the girl.

"It looks like a butterfly!" the girl said, as delighted as Piper. "But sparkly!"

"And they bring luck!" Piper answered. But with each step the girls took, more and more flutterfocuses circled them. Now the creatures seemed angry, baring enormous sharp teeth. "What's going on?" the Wishling cried. She squeezed Piper's hand, beginning to panic.

"I don't know," Piper said, keeping her voice calm. "These aren't like flutterfocuses at all! They're usually quite gentle, like all animals here!" Maybe if she could say something, do something, the flutterfocuses would return to their sweet normal ways. "Concentrate," Piper told herself, "concentrate. . . ."

Perhaps if they reached the plateau at the very top, edged with bright-colored bluebeezel flowers, the flutterfocuses would settle down.

Meanwhile, she held tight to the girl, pulling her up step by step. And finally, there was the peak, just within reach. She opened her mouth to tell the girl, "We're there," when a blinding light stopped her in her tracks.

"Oh, star apologies!" Vega had said, turning off the room light with a quick glance. Vega was very good at energy manipulation. But she wasn't very good at realizing when Piper was sleeping.

Thinking about it now, Piper wondered why the dream, which had begun so well, had turned so unpleasant. She didn't want to call it a nightmare. First of all, she'd dreamed it in the middle of day! Second, Piper believed that even the scariest, darkest dreams held meaning and could bring enlightenment. Piper felt sure this dream meant something important.

A Wishling girl . . . a difficult journey filled with danger and decisions . . . It was obvious, Piper saw now.

"I'm going on the next Wish Mission," she said aloud. It would be a successful mission, too, since in her dream, she and the girl had reached the mountaintop. Her smile faded slightly. Well, they had just about reached the top.

"What's going on?" Vega asked groggily, hearing Piper's voice.

"Nothing," Piper said quickly. Practical Vega wasn't one to believe in premonitions or dream symbols.

Once, while Vega slept, Piper had tiptoed over to watch her face for signs of emotion as she dreamed.

Vega had woken up and been totally creeped out to find Piper star inches away and staring. The girls generally got along, and they were friends—not best friends, but friends. And it helped for Piper to keep her insights to herself. She didn't want to upset the delicate balance.

Now, thinking about balance, she decided on a new bedtime visualization. She pictured a scale she'd seen in Wishling History class. It had a pan on each side, and when they were balanced, the pans were level. Adding weight to one would lift the other higher.

In her mind's eye, Piper placed a pebble first on one pan, then the other, again and again, so the scale moved up and down in a rhythm. Piper felt her head nodding in the same motion as she drifted off into another dream. . . .

As soon as the first glimmer of morning light landed on Piper's face, she opened her eyes. It was Star Kindness Day! She had a sense of expectation; something was about to happen.

She glanced at her Star-Zap. A holo-text was just coming through from Astra: LET'S ALL MEET AT THE RADIANT RECREATION CENTER BEFORE BREAKFAST.

Piper half groaned. She loved going to the rec center

for meditation class, but she doubted Astra wanted them all to sit still and think deeply. Most likely, she wanted to organize everyone for an early-morning star ball game. Well, Piper could be a good sport, so she made her way to the center, only to find the place deserted.

Then Leona holo-texted: I'M AT THE BAND SHELL. AREN'T WE SUPPOSED TO HAVE A PRE-BREAKFAST BAND REHEARSAL, WITH AN SD AUDIENCE?

Immediately, the Star-Zap buzzed again with a message from Cassie: NO! WE'RE SUPPOSED TO MEET AT LUMINOUS LIBRARY!

Not knowing what to do, Piper went to the band shell, then to the library, then searched across the quad for the Star Darlings. But everywhere she went turned out to be wrong. Her Star-Zap buzzed again and again, with message after message, louder and louder each time, until Piper shut it off with a flick of her wrist and realized she'd just turned off her alarm.

It was another dream.

Piper quickly entered it into her dream diary. She'd have to analyze it more, but it seemed to focus on mixed-up communications—not a good sign. Frowning, she looked toward Vega's part of the room.

"Are you going to the Celestial Café?" she called out.

Vega looked at her strangely. "Of course. It's breakfast."

"Just making sure," Piper said. "I still need to sparkle shower. So I'll see you there."

The sparkle shower made Piper's skin and hair glimmer brighter, and she felt its energy like a gentle boost of power. But the dream lingered, making her feel somehow off-kilter. She couldn't shake the feeling she'd show up at the cafeteria and everyone else would be having a special picnic breakfast at the orchard, or by the lake, or anywhere she wasn't.

By then, Piper was already late. No one would be concerned, though. Piper was frequently the last to arrive. She often needed to go back to her room to retrieve a forgotten item. But sometimes it was simply because she liked to take her time. Even now she paused to add a few more notes to her diary, while the dream was still fresh in her mind. It always helped to get everything down in writing, though she could usually remember details for at least a double starweek.

Even as a young Starling in Wee Constellation School, Piper could tell her mom specifics of her dreams, right down to what color socks she wore. Starmazingly, her mom sometimes wore the same color socks in her own dreams—and their actions often matched, too.

It had been hard to make friends growing up in the Gloom Flats; there weren't many girls Piper's age. The homes were spread so far apart it didn't make sense to have a Cosmic Transporter linking houses. So Piper had always felt an extra-special close connection to her mother.

When her granddad completed his Cycle of Life, Piper and her mom both dreamed that Piper and her older brother moved in with their grandmother on the other side of town. It seemed it was meant to be. Besides, her mom and dad were busy giving meditation workshops throughout Starland. It made sense for Piper and Finn to stay with their grandma. And Piper loved her grandmother's home, a mysterious old house floozels from everything, with a musty attic filled with odds and ends and a basement that echoed with eerie noises in the middle of the night. Piper found it all oddly comforting, even if classmates refused to visit. But now she had more classmates living on her floor than there were Starlings in all of Gloom Flats. And at least some of them—the Star Darlings—were waiting for her at the café.

★